Off limits . . .

Sally opened the door. A wooden stairway showed faintly in the light from the hall. It rose steeply up from the doorway and disappeared into the deeper darkness of what must be the attic. Sally could hear a tiny pattering sound somewhere up there. Her knees began to shake again, and she would have closed the door and scurried back downstairs had it not been for the doll. She might be up there, Sally told herself, she might.

Magic Elizabeth

Norma Kassirer
illustrated by Joe Krush

■ HarperTrophy®
A Division of HarperCollinsPublishers

for Karen and Sue

Originally published in 1966 by The Viking Press, Inc.

Magic Elizabeth
Copyright © 1966 by KSN Enterprises, LLC

Library of Congress Cataloging-in-Publication Data
Kassirer, Norma.
   Magic Elizabeth / by Norma Kassirer ; illustrated by Joe Krush.
    p.   cm.
   Summary: An eight-year-old girl is transported into the past while looking
for a lost doll in her aunt's memory chest.
   ISBN 0-06-440748-9 (pbk.)
   [1. Dolls—Fiction.   2. Time travel—Fiction.   I. Krush, Joe, ill.   II. Title.
PZ7.K156Mag   1999   98-45084
[Fic]—dc21   CIP
                                                      AC

Typography by Hilary Zarycky
2 3 4 5 6 7 8 9 10
❖
First Harper Trophy edition, 1999

Visit us on the World Wide Web!
http://www.harperchildrens.com

Contents

Rainy Night

IT ALL BEGAN ONE rainy night at the end of a summer.

"As if we didn't have enough troubles!" groaned Mrs. Chipley. "There it goes and rains on us!"

Sally, clinging to Mrs. Chipley's plump hand, was almost running to keep up with her. The bright feather on Mrs. Chipley's black hat, which had started out so proudly erect, had gradually wilted, and now drooped sadly down the back of that lady's stout neck. Sally's red suitcase, its handle firmly gripped by Mrs. Chipley's other hand, bumped in a steady rhythm against her right leg. But Mrs. Chipley strode purposefully on, as if she had no time to notice small discomforts.

The two of them had come all the way across the city on the bus, and during the ride the sky had darkened and the streetlights had bloomed all at once. High-piling storm clouds snuffed out the light of the round orange moon. As they stepped off the bus, the branches of the tall trees rattled like bones in the wind.

And now it was raining—a nasty, cold, stinging rain, mixed with wet leaves torn from the groaning trees. It splashed and flew about them as they hurried along the gloomy street, as if the faster they went the more they stirred up the fury of the night. Their coattails snapped behind them. Rain flew into Sally's eyes and even into her mouth, and it dribbled unpleasantly beneath the collar of her coat. Raindrops hitting a large mailbox echoed like drumbeats down the street. Sally's long red hair, fluttering bannerlike behind her, gave their small procession a brave look. And yet, Sally, at least, was not feeling brave at all. Quite the contrary.

"Troubles, troubles," Mrs. Chipley went on, "but it's a lucky thing your Aunt Sarah's come back to town just now when we need her."

"I don't remember her at all," panted Sally. "I was just a baby when she went away to California."

"Going back again, too, pretty soon, your ma tells me," said Mrs. Chipley. "Only came back here to sell the house. But never you mind, honey," she went on, without slackening her furious pace at all, "she's your own kin, and the only one you have here in town. I'm sure I didn't know what else to do but call her, what with your mom and dad away on that business trip, and we don't want to spoil it for them, and it's not as if you'd have to stay with your aunt forever. A few days and I'll have my daughter straightened around and come back. And it was your own ma left her name in case of an emergency."

"I wonder what she's like," Sally said. But Mrs. Chipley did not seem to hear her.

"And if my daughter's getting sick like that and five kids to take care of and her poor husband working day and night to keep food in their mouths isn't an emergency, then I'm sure I don't know what is!" Mrs. Chipley stopped so suddenly that Sally bumped into her. Mrs. Chipley, who was not very much taller than Sally herself, though a good deal bigger around, placed a steadying arm about Sally's shoulders and then peered up through the blowing rain at a street sign. She shook her head, sighed, and placed the red suitcase on the sidewalk.

"Land sakes, my glasses are all fogged over with wet," she said. "Can you read that sign, honey?"

Sally shaded her eyes and stood up on tiptoe, squinting to make out the letters on the sign in the uncertain gleam of a streetlight. The blowing shadows of tree branches came and went over the words on the sign. The letters wavered, grew taller, then shorter, then seemed to disappear entirely.

"It says Forest Road," she said at last.

"Can't hear you, dearie, your voice is gone all husky. Hope you don't go getting a cold now on top of everything else."

"Forest Road," said Sally, more strongly this time.

"This is it," said Mrs. Chipley, nodding vigorously. "Forest Road. Come along, honey." And picking up the suitcase, she led the way down Aunt Sarah's street. Sally's hand crept back into hers. "Now watch the numbers on the houses," Mrs. Chipley said. "It's eighty-two we want. Your young eyes are better than mine."

"But there aren't any houses," said Sally, for as far as she could see, all down the street on either side, were buildings, tall buildings, the light from their windows streaming out into the blowing street. Like the letters on the street sign, the buildings seemed to waver behind the lashing curtains of rain. A leaf danced in one of the streams of light for a moment, and then vanished into the darkness.

"It's a funny sort of street for your aunt to live on, all right," said Mrs. Chipley. "All these apartment buildings. But if it's Forest Road, it's got to be your aunt Sarah's street. You sure you read that sign right, honey?"

"Yes," said Sally. The hand clinging to Mrs. Chipley's grew suddenly very cold. Mrs. Chipley looked down as if she'd noticed it too. She squeezed Sally's hand gently. "There, honey," she said, "you're not scared, are you?"

Sally shook her head. But she *was* scared. She was scared of the strange dark street with the rain splashing in the gutters, of the wind-blown shadows shivering over the walk, of the tall buildings looming over them and seeming to watch them with the glittering eyes of their windows. And of her aunt, whose street this was, and whom she did not know at all.

Mrs. Chipley squeezed her hand again. "Now, don't you be scared!" she said kindly. "Everything'll look better tomorrow morning. Just you wait and see. Why, you're no baby! You're eight years old, aren't you?"

"Almost nine," Sally answered.

"Almost nine! Well now! That's too old to be scared of your own great-aunt. Why, when I talked to her on the phone, she said—she said—well—'you may bring the girl over' was what she said, and I'll tell you, the connection wasn't good what with this storm coming on, so I couldn't hear her real good, but I'd say, yes, I'd say she sounded kind. Yes, that's what she sounded—*kind!* It was hard to tell, of course, but if it'd been a better connection, she'd have sounded just as kind as could be, I'm sure of that."

Mrs. Chipley's words, blown back to Sally by the wind as they continued hurrying along, seemed somehow as cold and unreassuring as the rain that accompanied them.

"Watch for the numbers now, sweetie! Oof! This rain! We'll be soaked to the skin for sure and poor Mrs. Chipley has to run right back to the bus stop to get the train for my daughter's on time. Can't even stop for a cup of tea, and I expect your Aunt Sarah'll want me to. Trouble, trouble."

"Ninety," said Sally.

"What's that, dearie?"

"It says 'ninety' on that building."

"There we go, then. It'll be on this side of the street and not so far off at that." Mrs. Chipley, to Sally's relief, had slowed down. "You don't suppose your aunt lives in one of these buildings, do you?" she asked, looking up at one of them. "Can't be, though. It's a house she came back to sell. An old house."

I'm scared, thought Sally. Take me with you, Mrs. Chipley, I won't be any trouble, I promise. But she didn't say any of it. "Eighty-eight," she said instead. "Eighty-six."

"Eighty-six! Oh, we're close, all right! What's this?" Mrs. Chipley stopped. Sally stood still beside her, staring where Mrs. Chipley was pointing. "What's this?" she asked again.

"It's a house," whispered Sally. She knew now what it meant to feel your heart sink. Hers seemed to be somewhere around her toes.

For the peaked roof of what must be a house could just be seen above the top of a line of tall scraggly bushes that formed an untidy hedge along the edge of the sidewalk. It was the only house, as far as they could see, on the entire street.

As they stared, they heard a creaking sound and saw, almost hidden by the overgrown bushes, a pretty little wrought-iron gate moving slowly back and forth and back and forth in the wind, screeching quite plaintively as it went.

It seemed to Sally, at that moment, the saddest sound she had ever heard.

"What's those numbers on the gate, dearie?"

Sally bent her head to peer at them. She put a hand upon the gate to hold it still. The metal was cold and wet. She shivered. The numbers on the gate said "eighty-two," just as she had feared. She told Mrs. Chipley.

"This is it, then, honey. Come along." And Mrs. Chipley, still holding Sally's hand, pushed the gate open with the suitcase she held in her other hand, and led the way along a path into Aunt Sarah's garden.

Behind them, the gate began its monotonous complaint again.

"The house is dark," said Sally, and her voice was trembling.

"Never mind that," said Mrs. Chipley briskly. "This is it, all right. I expect she's somewhere at the back of the house where we can't see, no doubt in the kitchen hotting up that tea," she added longingly.

It looked, Sally thought in despair, like a witch's house. She was suddenly afraid that she might begin to cry. Don't you *dare*, she ordered herself. Don't you *cry!*

"A shame to have to refuse that cup of tea," Mrs. Chipley was murmuring, shaking her head.

A Strange Lady

THE HOUSE WAS DARK INDEED, both inside and out, so far as they could see. The mean, peaked roof was faintly illuminated by a streetlight. Stiff wooden lace edged the lower roof of a large porch, and lacy shadows trembled over the front of the house. A broken chimney pointed toward the sky exactly like a long, skinny finger. And the garden—if it could be called a garden—the garden was full of shadows that leaped, darted, appeared and disappeared, and followed one another in shuddering lines along the grass. Besides, there was a shutter on a creaky hinge playing an eerie accompaniment to the unhappy tune of the gate, and there hung, over all, a damp, musty toadstool smell.

Coldness shivered along the back of Sally's neck as they climbed the porch steps. "You'd think she'd have the porch light on," complained Mrs. Chipley, stumbling on one of the broken steps. "What with her knowing we're coming and all. But never mind, maybe something's gone wrong with the electricity."

Sally held her breath as Mrs. Chipley raised

her hand and pulled the old-fashioned bell beside the door. "Bell works, though," she said, "funny old thing. Must be an old house, all right." The wind howled and sighed and rattled the windows of the old house. Sally could not imagine this terrible house under any other conditions and wondered if perhaps the wind always behaved like this around here. Beyond the moaning of the wind and the thudding of her heart, she could hear the faint tinkle of the bell inside. She could hear it echoing through—what? What sort of rooms could there be beyond this door? How different her own house seemed to her at this moment. She could not seem to remember it except as bright and cheerful, with sunlight streaming in at the windows, and her mother singing as she worked in the kitchen or in her little sewing room with the bouquets of violets printed on the curtains. Oh, how she wished that she could turn right now and run as fast as she could, down the steps, along the path, and out of that shadowy garden, and somehow, somehow, back to her own safe, familiar home.

But, of course, there would be no one there at all. There was nothing she could do but wait here on the porch while Mrs. Chipley impatiently yanked at the bell once more.

Something moved inside the house this

time. Footsteps were approaching the door. A light suddenly went on inside.

"There, you see!" said Mrs. Chipley triumphantly. She reached down and squeezed Sally's cold hand.

The big door slowly creaked open. Inside, standing in the harsh orange light from an overhead bulb, stood a very old lady. Her hair, pulled back from her wrinkled face, was gray, and she was dressed entirely in black. Though she was taller than Mrs. Chipley by far, her face seemed very close to Sally, for she stood in a bent-over position, holding one hand pressed against her back. Sally blinked and stared up at her. It seemed to her that the lady was scowling down at them, though it may have been that she was attempting to smile, an exercise which her face seemed unaccustomed to performing.

The lady was perfectly still, except for the rippling of her black dress in the wind. She seemed to Sally for a moment exactly like a statue. As they stared at each other, the lady raised a hand to her gray hair, to protect it from the wind.

"How do you do," she said. Her voice sounded every bit as rusty as the voice of the iron gate.

"How d'do," answered Mrs. Chipley politely.

"Hello," whispered Sally.

"You must be Mrs. Chipley," said the lady, "and Sally," she added, looking down at her.

Sally nodded, gulped, and attempted what turned out to be a weak smile.

The thin, long-nosed face of the strange lady seemed to have settled ages ago into a permanent frown. When her mouth moved briefly in what was perhaps another try at a smile, Sally felt as if it was not the gate but the odd smile that creaked.

"Well, Sally, I'm your aunt Sarah. You'd both better step in out of the rain. You'll catch your death out there."

"No, no, I'll be on my way back to the bus stop," said Mrs. Chipley, "now I see Sally's going to be all right," she added rather doubtfully. (She doesn't like Aunt Sarah either, thought Sally.) "Yes, I've got a train to make tonight, what with my poor daughter sick and all, and oh, here's Sally's suitcase—everything she'll need for a few days, pajamas and her toothbrush, a hairbrush and a nice new pink comb we got her at the drugstore—couldn't find the old one, though we looked high and low—"

"Yes, yes, Mrs. Chipley," said Aunt Sarah, sounding impatient. "Sally, take your suitcase and step inside, please. There is a draft from the door, and I'm afraid Shadow will catch cold."

Shadow? wondered Sally. Who was Shadow? But she did not dare to ask.

"Thank you, Mrs. Chipley," said Aunt Sarah firmly, for Mrs. Chipley stood hesitating on the brink of the porch steps. "Thank you for bringing Sally. She'll be all right now."

A small tendril of hope sprouted in the region of Sally's heart. Maybe Mrs. Chipley wouldn't leave her after all.

But, "Good-bye, then, honey," said Mrs. Chipley, moving impulsively back toward the door again and enfolding Sally in her comfortable clasp. Sally flung her arms around the plump neck. Oh, take me with you, she yearned to cry. Oh, please. But again she did not say it. Mrs. Chipley kissed her cheek and then straightened up, brushing at her own eyes as she did so. "There goes old Mrs. Chipley crying. I'm that sentimental," she said to Aunt Sarah, who did not make any comment at this news. Mrs. Chipley bent to kiss Sally again, and whispered in her ear, "Don't you worry, honey, everything'll be all right, and Mrs. Chipley'll hurry back as quick as she can." Then, pressing Sally's hand, she turned and hurried off down the steps into the rain and darkness.

Aunt Sarah had not mentioned tea at all. Why didn't she? thought Sally angrily. Poor

Mrs. Chipley, at least she'd have liked to be offered some.

"All right," said Aunt Sarah sharply. "Hurry in, please."

Sally stepped hesitantly into the hallway of the strange house. The door swung closed behind her. From somewhere in the darkness, which seemed to fill all the house beyond the orange light, there came a most curious sound, a sort of bad-tempered yowl, which caused Sally to start in surprise and fright. This was followed by a petulant cough.

"There now, you see," said Aunt Sarah, "poor Shadow's coughing! This house is simply freezing. Come here, Shadow."

And out of the darkness, into the pool of light, there stepped a very large, very black cat. The cat narrowed its eyes at Sally, flattened its ears, and hissed.

"Is that Shadow?" asked Sally.

"Yes," said Aunt Sarah. "That is indeed poor Shadow."

The cat, golden eyes gleaming up at Sally in an unfriendly way, rubbed up against Aunt Sarah, who reached down to touch the top of its black head with her long, skinny fingers. With her stooped figure and her gray hair pulled tightly back into a bun, she looked just like a witch. One thin strand, perhaps loosened by the wind Sally had brought in with her, straggled over her hollow cheek.

Sally felt sure that she'd never be staying here if her mother knew what it was really like.

She was suddenly terribly tired.

Another Sally

SALLY MOVED UNCERTAINLY into the hall and, not knowing what else to do, set down her suitcase.

"Sally!" cried her aunt, so sharply that Sally jumped. "Stay right where you are! I should think at your age you would know better! Step back, please! Step back!" Sally, bewildered and unhappy, did so. "Look," said her aunt, pointing to a spot on the rug just in front of Sally's feet.

Sally looked, but it was very difficult to see anything in the dim hallway. "Dirt!" said her aunt impatiently. "On my rug! We're going to have to make some rules, and the first one is"—she spoke very sharply and distinctly— *"Wipe your feet on the mat before coming in!"*

"I'm sorry," whispered Sally, but her aunt brushed past her, opened the door of a small narrow closet near the front door, and brought out a broom. She began to sweep the rug angrily, as if she wanted to sweep Sally out too. Sally half expected her to leap onto the broom, with the black cat behind, and soar away into the night. And I wish she would, thought Sally. Her eyes misted with tears as she wiped her feet on the mat near the door.

Her aunt was muttering as she swept, as if she were talking to herself. "Have to keep this house clean!" she said, brushing furiously at one spot on the rug. "Girl came in and cleaned it. Took her wages and never came back." She bent, one hand pressed to her back, and peered at the spot. Then she sighed, straightened as if she found it difficult to do so, and went on sweeping harder than ever. "How I'm going to manage everything myself, I don't know! Can't get anyone who wants to work nowadays!" Swish, swish, whispered the broom, more slowly now. It seemed to be growing tired.

She doesn't want me here, thought Sally in despair. Now she has me *and* the house to take care of and she doesn't like it.

She stood on the mat, feeling awkward and very lonely, while her aunt continued to sweep the rug. She felt a lump beginning in her throat, and her feet were wet and uncomfortable. She sneezed.

At last her aunt looked up from her sweeping. "Well," she said, "don't just stand there! Come in, come in, if your feet are clean. Here, hold them up and I'll see." Sally leaned against the door frame, and slowly raised one foot and then the other, while Aunt Sarah bent to peer at them. Her aunt snorted, straightened up, and put the broom back in the closet. Sally stood listening to the steady drip of rain from the porch roof, which made her conscious of the deep quiet of the dimly lit house. She shivered.

Aunt Sarah turned back to her. "Why you didn't wear rubbers, I don't know!" she grumbled.

"It wasn't raining when we left," whispered Sally. But her aunt did not seem to hear her.

"You have slippers in there?" She indicated the suitcase. Sally nodded.

"Take them out." Sally opened the suitcase with nervous fingers, found her fuzzy pink slippers, removed her shoes, and put the slippers on. It did feel better.

"Leave the shoes on the mat," ordered her aunt. "You'll be getting a cold next and then what will I do with you?"

When Sally had placed the shoes side by side on the mat, her aunt said, "All right, you may come with me."

She followed Aunt Sarah through the musty-smelling hall to a larger closet at the back of the hall. It was filled with what looked to Sally like a number of long, dusty black coats. Her aunt reached into the closet, brought out a hanger, and, without a word, handed it to Sally. Then, seeing that Sally still wore her coat, she snatched the hanger back and said impatiently, "No more dawdling now, Sally, take your coat off." Sally removed her coat and her hat, and stood awkwardly holding them, wondering whether her aunt would give her the hanger or would place the coat on it herself.

Aunt Sarah touched the coat with her long fingers, and then hastily drew them back. "Wet!" she pronounced, as if Sally were responsible for something very bad. "Well, give it to me." She sighed heavily. "It'll have to go over the sink." Sally handed the coat to her. Holding it with two fingers, as if trying to touch it as little as possible, Aunt Sarah placed it on the hanger. "You carry the hat," she said, giving that rain-soaked object a disdainful look.

Sally followed her, holding the hat as if she were comforting it. She felt very sorry for that small, unwanted blue hat, which had already dripped some rain on Aunt Sarah's rug.

They made their way down a long shadowy passageway leading from the front hall toward the back of the house. Sally was just beginning to feel a tiny bit better as the slippers warmed her feet when from somewhere ahead of them there came a high-pitched whistle. Sally stumbled in alarm and her hand reached out toward the wall to support herself. Her fingers leaped back when they encountered something soft.

She turned her head with an effort, for her neck ached with tension. She was looking into the gleaming glass eyes of a stuffed owl, sitting on a little shelf attached to the wall. The whistling rose higher. Sally felt quite faint with terror.

"Teakettle," snapped her aunt, who had not stopped.

It took a moment for Sally to collect herself, and then she hurried on after her aunt, not wanting to be left behind in this dark hall with the staring owl.

Aunt Sarah pushed open a door at the end of the hall. The whistling grew louder. Sally followed her into the kitchen.

Tall cupboards of dark wood, with knots that

stared down like eyes, loomed over them. And there was an enormous stone fireplace, quite empty, and so huge that Sally could easily have walked into it. She had never before seen a fireplace of this size, and she wondered how it would look with a fire burning in it. This was a very strange sort of house indeed. Hearing a faint ticking sound, she looked up and saw upon the mantel of the fireplace, along with a number of blue-and-white pitchers and plates, a little clock shaped like a church. Its pendulum was a small gold bell in the steeple, which moved quickly back and forth. It was a friendly looking clock with a matter-of-fact sort of voice, and you almost could not look at it without smiling. Aunt Sarah hurried to the stove and moved the kettle, and Sally, looking at the clock, began to feel just the tiniest bit better. There were appetizing odors and comforting bubbling sounds coming from the stove. It was warmer here in the kitchen.

Aunt Sarah hung Sally's coat on a hook above the sink, and Sally stood beside the long wooden table in the center of the room, listening to the steady drip, drip of water from the coat. She timidly placed her hat upon the table, and her aunt's long fingers reached out and snatched it up. The hat appeared upon a hook beside the coat.

Sally stood without speaking in the strange kitchen, while her aunt quickly removed pans from the stove and filled dishes and glasses. If she had not been so frightened, Sally would have offered to help, as she did at home with her mother. But she had no idea how she ought to behave with this strange lady, and so she said nothing at all.

"Waited dinner for you," said her aunt's gruff voice. "Had enough for Mrs. Chipley too. I thought she'd at least want a cup of tea before she left." She indicated the teakettle now quietly bubbling to itself. "But everyone's in a hurry hurry hurry these days. Sit down." Sally looked up in surprise to see that Aunt Sarah was already seated at the other end of the table, where Sally could not see her face clearly. The kitchen was lit only by the low blue flame of the gas stove, and a rather dusty bulb in a paper shade hanging over the middle of the table. Near Sally was placed a dish of peas and potatoes and chicken. Since she and Mrs. Chipley had eaten dinner before leaving home, she was not at all hungry, but she did not dare to mention it. She sat down, pushing back a chair which stood near the table. The chair legs squeaked over the linoleum, and Sally looked anxiously across at the shadowed figure, fearing that Aunt Sarah might say she was scratching the floor. But Aunt Sarah said nothing.

In fact she did not talk at all during the meal. Shadow wove his way under the table, brushing against Sally's legs from time to time, and then darting across the kitchen floor. Sally could hear something bumping lightly along the floor, as if he were pushing it with his paw, but she could not see what it was.

When Sally at last put her knife and fork across her plate and looked up, her aunt's harsh voice spoke from the other end of the table. "Didn't eat much, Sally. Doesn't your mother make you eat?"

"Yes," said Sally in a small voice. "But I'm not very hungry," she added bravely, her voice rising to an unfamiliar squeak on the last word.

Aunt Sarah stood up. It seemed to take some effort to unfold herself from the chair. She leaned across the table, one hand pressed against her back, and the other flattened on the table. How crooked her fingers were, Sally thought, staring at them. She looked up at her aunt's face, which had appeared in the cone of light cast by the hanging bulb. It looked annoyed, or angry. Perhaps both. "I think then," her aunt said, "that you'd better go up to bed. Little girls who can't eat belong in bed."

Sally swallowed and looked miserably down at her hands in her lap.

"Well," said her aunt, walking around the table to her. She put a bony hand on Sally's shoulder. "Let's go," she said gruffly.

Sally stood up and followed her through the pantry and into the hall once more, where she picked up her suitcase. Aunt Sarah had switched on some more lights, and Sally could now see that the entrance to what must be the living room was hung with the oddest curtains she had ever seen. They were not really curtains at all, but rather a series of tiny colored beads on long strings, hanging close together to form a sort of screen or curtain. The beads moved and made a gentle clicking sound as Sally and her aunt passed. Sally could just glimpse dimly beyond the bead curtains the curving backs of chairs and sofas which looked very old. Their gentle shapes seemed comforting. Aunt Sarah was all straight sharp lines, and not comforting in the least. And Sally heard, too, as they passed, from somewhere deep inside the room, a very delicate musical sound, faint and rather trembling.

"The melodeon. Always does that when the floor shakes. Used to play it when I was your age." Sally was too astounded at such a wealth of information from Aunt Sarah to ask what a melodeon was. But it sounded as if it must be something very graceful and beautiful.

She was surprised to see, now that the lights were on, that a white marble angel stood on a post at the foot of the curving staircase. The angel held a twisted orange bulb like a candle flame in one hand. She was smiling gently and looking out somewhere beyond the front door, perhaps, thought Sally, to where her parents were. She touched the angel's cold bare foot as she passed. Shadow followed along behind them, almost as silent as a real shadow.

The stairway was longer than any Sally had ever climbed before. It went on and on, twisting and turning, and each time that Sally thought they must be at the top there was another turn, and more stairs, leading up and up. What a strange house, she thought again.

Sally had become aware of a very loud ticking sound that increased in volume as they went up the stairs. At last, finding herself in a long hallway lined with many doors on either side, she saw, down at the far end near a back stairway, a solemn-looking grandfather clock as tall as the ceiling. There was nothing friendly about this clock, as there had been about the little kitchen clock, and Sally stared at it in respectful awe. She had never seen one like it before, and she was astounded by its size and deep voice and by the flashing of its pendulum behind the glass cover. The clock seemed to be announcing that in this part of the house, at least, *it* was in charge.

The floor of the hall was covered by a gray carpet patterned with enormous red flowers. Shadow sat on one of the flowers and gave a huge yawn, which ended in a high, petulant meow. The sound echoed down the hallway, and Sally shivered and began to yawn too. She was very tired, almost too tired to care about anything—even when her aunt opened one of the doors that lined the hall and showed her into the room that would be hers. It was a very pretty room, the prettiest Sally had ever seen, its furniture painted pale blue, its brass bed covered with a ruffled yellow spread. The yellow curtains at an open window snapped in the wind. Sally placed her suitcase on the floor next to the bed. She felt too shy to say, "This is a very pretty room," which was what she was thinking.

"Now how did that get open?" said her aunt. One of the two windows in the room was slightly open. Aunt Sarah walked over to it and shut it. She looked angrily at the wet curtains.

While her aunt was frowning at the curtains, Sally looked up at an oil painting that hung over a little green marble fireplace. It was a picture of a girl about Sally's own age, with long red hair, a sprinkle of freckles over the nose, and round greenish eyes. She wore a yellow bonnet tied with ribbons beneath her chin, a long pale blue dress with three layers of ruffles, and high-buttoned shoes. The girl was holding a rag doll on her lap and she was looking down at it as if she loved it very much. The doll's hair was long and was made of what seemed to be thick strands of golden thread. It had a painted pink mouth curled into a smile at the corners. The eyes were a deep blue, the pleasant shape of watermelon seeds, and painted on with a very thin brush so that each golden eyelash showed. The doll was wearing a long blue dress and small high-buttoned shoes, and even a yellow bonnet, exactly like those worn by its mistress. Its hands were tucked into a tiny white fur muff. It was the most adorable doll Sally had ever seen, and in less than a moment she had fallen in love with it.

"I see," said Aunt Sarah, pointing with a sharp finger that seemed to slice the soft air in the pretty room, "that you're looking at the picture."

Sally nodded.

"That was a girl who lived in this house a long time ago. She must have been about your age when the picture was painted. This was her room." She lowered her arm abruptly, as if she were a mechanical toy that had run down, looked proudly about the room, and straightened the round rag rug which Sally had mussed in walking over it. "Some of those old things in the picture are stored in the attic," she murmured.

But Sally was staring at the picture.

The girl in the picture was smiling, so that a dimple deepened in her left cheek. Sally had not noticed that before. It was almost as if the girl's expression had changed, just a little, since she had first looked at the picture.

Sally's fingers touched the dimple in her own cheek. Why, she looks just like *me!* she thought in astonishment.

"You resemble the girl in the picture quite remarkably," Aunt Sarah was saying. "They called her Sally too."

Aunt Sarah showed Sally where the bathroom was, right next door to her room, gave her a pink towel and washcloth, and then came back to the bedroom with her. While Sally began unpacking her suitcase, her aunt straightened the curtains, turned back the yellow spread to reveal a bright patchwork quilt beneath it, and moved a vase carefully into the very center of a little table that stood beside the bed. She cleared her throat several times as if she were going to say something and then, quite abruptly, she touched Sally on the shoulder, said, "Well, good night," and out she went, with Shadow following. As the door was closing behind them, Shadow looked back. The golden glitter of his eyes seemed to linger in the room long after the door had closed.

Mysterious sounds from the darkness outside invaded the quiet room. Branches rubbed against the walls of the old house. Trees creaked and groaned in the wind, and a sudden splash of rain hit the window as if a hand had thrown it. And yet Sally felt oddly comforted by the pretty room and its oil painting. She smiled shyly up at the portrait of the other Sally and her doll. She wondered what the other Sally would think if she could see her placing her clothes in the top drawer of the blue painted chest.

She looks nice, she thought. I think I would have liked her.

But I don't like Aunt Sarah, and I don't like Shadow, she told herself as she put on her pajamas. I don't like them at all.

Before getting into bed she looked around the room, at the wallpaper, sprinkled with tiny bouquets of pink flowers that reminded her of the violets on the curtains in her mother's sewing room. A small white desk held a feather pen stuck into a blue bowl filled with tiny white pebbles; the dainty blue chair next to it seemed to be the very chair upon which the other Sally was seated in the picture.

She sat down in the chair and tried to imagine how it must have felt to be that other Sally, so long ago. She looked up at the painting, and she placed her hands just like the other Sally's hands and pretended that she was holding the soft cottony body of the little doll.

As she went to sleep that night, with the patchwork quilt pulled up to her chin, almost the last thing she was conscious of was the painting. The rain had almost stopped. Moonlight suddenly flooded the room. In the silvery light the picture seemed to spring to life. In just another moment, if Sally could keep her eyes open, the other Sally might step down by way of the mantel and enter the room she had left so long ago . . .

But the very last thing she heard, just as she was dropping off to sleep, was a mournful yowl, which might have been the wind, or perhaps Shadow, somewhere in the darkness beyond her window.

She woke up once that night, shivering, from a dream in which Aunt Sarah, wearing a pointed black hat and a great billowing black cloak, was riding upon the back of an enormous Shadow. Closer and closer they came and closer and closer—

She lay awake in the dark for a long time,

trembling, and in the strange moaning blackness, with the trees beating like wings at the mysterious old house, it seemed quite possible to her that Aunt Sarah might indeed be a witch.

But when she fell asleep again at last, it was to dream that she was playing with the other Sally and her doll upon the round rag rug beside the bed, and that the sun was streaming in through the windows.

Alone

THERE WAS SOMETHING COLD on Sally's forehead. Her eyes flew open in alarm. Looming over her was Aunt Sarah's sharp-nosed face; her thin hand rested upon Sally's forehead. Something moved at the foot of the bed, and Sally's eyes turned quickly to confront Shadow, seated at her feet. He narrowed his eyes and looked back at her, unblinking. For just a moment it was like another bad dream. Sally thought that she might scream, but she found that her throat had gone so dry that she could never have managed it. Which, after all, was probably just as well. For what good would it do?

Her aunt, seeing Sally staring up at her, quickly drew her hand away.

Sally immediately closed her eyes again, hoping that Aunt Sarah would think she was sleeping and go away.

But, "Sally," her aunt whispered.

Sally did not answer for a time, but at last, feeling Aunt Sarah still standing there, she slowly opened her eyes and looked up at her. This close, with the morning sun filling the room, she could see that Aunt Sarah's eyes, like Shadow's, were pale green.

Aunt Sarah reached again toward Sally's forehead. Sally turned her head away and stared at the flower-sprinkled wall. The moving shadows of leaves came and went over the little bouquets. Aunt Sarah snatched her hand back. "Good morning," she said sharply. "Do you feel all right? Your head seems warm and you look quite flushed. I'm not used to children, you understand."

"I'm all right," Sally answered stiffly, turning her head to look up at Aunt Sarah. Her voice, to her surprise, sounded rather hoarse. She tried to stifle a cough, but Aunt Sarah noticed it.

She looked sharply at Sally, who looked back, unmoving. Something flickered in Aunt Sarah's eyes. If it had been anyone else, Sally would have thought it was concern, or kindness. But since it was Aunt Sarah—Sally turned her head away again. I hope I'm not getting a cold, thought Sally, remembering the rain the night before. Then she'll really be mad at me.

Her eyes moved to the windows. A maple tree was looking in through both of them. She wondered if it could be one tree. If so, it was a very large one. She blinked at the brilliant gold-and-green light that glittered in the moving leaves. Between two swaying branches, she could see what looked like the corner of an old barn.

She raised herself on one elbow and looked up at her aunt, seeing her now through a moving blur of light. She blinked again. "Is that a barn?" she asked, before she could help herself. She didn't really like to ask Aunt Sarah anything at all.

"Yes," said her aunt. "This house used to be a farmhouse a long time ago, at the edge of a little town called Forest Valley."

Sally looked at the painting above the fireplace.

"Yes," said her aunt, following her gaze to the painting. "This was all country around here when she lived here. None of these buildings—" She waved an arm to indicate the apartment buildings on all sides of them. "But breakfast is almost ready," she said. "We'll see you downstairs shortly." Aunt Sarah turned and walked out the door.

Shadow growled low in his throat, flicked a glance at Sally, and jumped off the bed to follow Aunt Sarah out.

As soon as they had gone, Sally jumped out of bed and ran to a window to look out. She could see now that it was indeed one enormous maple tree that showed at both windows. The tree seemed absorbed in shaking raindrops from its leaves. One leaf lay like a hand against a windowpane. Sally placed her hand over it. A wide margin of the sharp-edged leaf showed all around her hand, which looked quite small against it. How large the leaf was! She had never seen one so big. She supposed that the tree, like the house, must be very old.

She peered down through the moving leaves into what seemed at first to be a rippling green sea. Her room was at the back of the house, and she was looking down into what must once have been the garden. Now it was a blowing field of foxtails, tall grass, and Queen Anne's lace. Blue and yellow butterflies rocked like tiny boats on the billowing green. The fur of the foxtails flared in the sun. Raindrops sparkled on the grass and weeds. The leaves of the apple trees— there were a number of them—were still shiny with rain.

Tall apartment buildings rose on either side and at the far end of the yard. How stiffly the red-brick buildings, their windows silver with raindrops, stood there enclosing the leaping garden. They might have been forbidding it to move on any further. For it seemed that the wild tangly growth out there meant to do so if it could. Already it was lapping up the sides of the apartment buildings in vines, perhaps planning to creep over the top of them to the other side.

The old barn slanted alarmingly beneath the vines, which nearly covered it. Its roof was sinking in the middle, as if the vines were working from inside too.

A row of pine trees at the back of the yard might have been the beginning of a deep forest, had it not been for the tall building just behind. The vines were busy there too, winding up into the pine trees and dragging their branches down. They had even crawled into the apple trees, so that the green-and-yellow apples looked as if they were growing from the vines. Bushes were bowed down by them. Even the grass and weeds were woven together in some places into little knotted bouquets.

How pretty it all was! If Aunt Sarah's appearance had been like a bad dream, this was certainly a good one.

Sally leaned on the windowsill and gazed down, feeling indeed as if she might be dreaming.

In all that moving green, a tiny flash of red caught Sally's eye just then in the crack between the barn doors. She pressed her face against the glass and stared out at it. She wondered what it could be.

How she longed to be out there, feeling the breeze lifting her hair. She turned her cheek to the cool glass, imagining how it would be. She wanted to wade through that sea of green, the foxtails tickling her knees. She wanted to peek into the barn, perhaps even go inside. What had it been like when the other Sally lived here? she wondered.

How quiet the room seemed behind her. The furniture was as stiff as the buildings. The only movement in the room was the flicker of leaf shadow over the walls and floor. Only the ticking of the grandfather clock in the hall broke the absolute stillness of the house.

Just then there came a metallic clatter from the kitchen, reminding her that Aunt Sarah was waiting. She sighed and turned from the window. Maybe after breakfast she could go outside, if she could work up the courage to ask.

They ate breakfast at the big round table in the dining room, seated in high-backed gilded chairs with red velvet seats. Sally thought that they were quite a lot like thrones. Beside them, on a shelf beneath a bay window, stood a pot of tall ferns, looking like a miniature forest.

"Bought that the first day I was here," Aunt Sarah explained. "Shadow likes something green in the house, to nibble." And sure enough, just then Shadow, who had been cleaning his paws beneath the table, jumped up on the shelf and delicately nipped at a frond of fern.

Beyond the window, at the end of the rippling

garden, Sally could see the row of pine trees, seeming even more like a real forest than they had from upstairs, for from where she was sitting she could see nothing of the building behind them through the thick branches. How dark and mysterious they looked, even by daylight!

They had very little to say to each other during breakfast, although Sally was bursting with questions such as, What is that red I saw in the barn? and Can't I please play outside? But every time that she peeked across the table at Aunt Sarah's stern-lipped face, her courage failed her.

Sally sneezed.

Her aunt looked up. "That doesn't sound good," she said. "You'd better stay inside this morning, Sally. You may play in the parlor or anywhere you like in the house, if you are careful not to break anything, but you'd better not go into the attic. It's much too dusty and dirty up there." And she stood up, excused herself and went into the kitchen.

Sally looked up from her plate, pushed her chair back, stood up and wandered into the big parlor that she had glimpsed the night before through the bead curtains.

As she came into the room, she surprised Shadow, who jumped into the air and skidded across the shiny floor on a small rug, giving a startled "m-row" as he went. Sally clapped her hand to her mouth, and out came a sound that was very much like a strangled laugh.

"Cats," said Aunt Sarah's voice, "are very dignified, and do not like to be laughed at." Sally looked up to see her standing, a broom in one hand, just beyond the bead curtains in the front hall. Shadow walked through the curtains to her, and Aunt Sarah picked him up. Sally could see the glitter of his fiery eyes in the dim hallway, and then both of them disappeared. Tears started in Sally's eyes and blurred the hanging beads so that they looked like the glitter of Shadow's eyes, endlessly repeated. She angrily brushed the tears away. "I didn't mean anything wrong," she whispered. But she'd done it again. There seemed to be no pleasing Aunt Sarah. She doesn't like me any more than I like her, she thought. She's afraid I'll hurt her house, or her cat.

"I'm going out for a short time," called Aunt Sarah, reappearing so suddenly behind the bead curtains that Sally jumped. Her aunt was wearing a hat, and was drawing white gloves over her fingers. "I'll leave Shadow with you," she said and she was gone, the door opening to let a flood of sunlight into the hall, and then closing with a soft thud that was like the sound of darkness returning to the hall. Sally ran to a window and peeked out. She watched her aunt go down the path, through the little iron gate, and then she watched as her aunt's profile, beneath the black hat, sailed grimly over the tops of the bushes.

Sally turned and faced the room. She was alone, she thought. "I'm all alone," she said aloud, trying her voice to see how it sounded in the still room. It sounded very small indeed, and rather frightened besides. How very big the house felt suddenly. The long beaded strings of the curtain, which had been disturbed by the opening and closing of the door, still clicked softly together. Sally sat down on a tiny flowered stool in front of the fireplace, which was of green marble like the one in her room, only much larger. As she did so, she heard again the tiny tremble of music she had heard the night before in the hall. And her eyes found, between two velvet-draped windows, what must be the melodeon.

Sally walked over to it. It was a very pretty and graceful instrument, rather like a small piano. Its wood was highly polished, and smelled faintly of lemon. She shyly touched one of the yellowed keys, and the tinkly musical note flew lightly about the room. What a pretty thing it is, she thought. Imagine it belonging

to Aunt Sarah. For it was as unlike her as anything could be, very dainty and possessing a most beautiful voice.

She turned from the melodeon to look at the rest of the room, and the music died away. She became aware too of the sounds of traffic in the street, cars and trucks passing, horns honking and heels clicking—loud for a time, then fading away to be replaced by other sounds. She thought again that the furniture looked very old, as if it must remember a time when the noises outside were quite different. Most of it was upholstered in some kind of velvet, worn dull in spots and shiny in others. The wood that framed many of the chairs and love seats was carved with flowers and bunches of grapes. Maybe it had looked like this when the other Sally lived here, she thought. The gas jet in the fireplace was on, and the line of flickering blue flames made a comforting bubbling sound in the otherwise quiet room.

Two tall cupboards with rounded glass fronts stood against one wall, looking like a pair of prim old-fashioned ladies. Sally walked across the room to peer into them, wondering at their contents. She had never been in a house like this before. Everything, even Aunt Sarah, seemed to have come from another time.

One cupboard held a set of teacups and saucers, and beside them was another set exactly the same, except that these were doll-sized. She wondered if they had belonged to the other Sally, and she longed to touch them, but did not dare to open the cupboard. One of the tiny cups, she could see, had lost a handle. The cups, brushed with gold inside, were so thin that she could see through them, as if they were really the ghosts of cups used here long ago. She imagined the rustle of the ladies' long skirts as their hands gently lifted the fragile cups. Perhaps the other Sally had sat on the fireplace stool, holding her doll and watching them, and the room was lit by candles—no—she looked at the line of blue flames in the fireplace—gaslights, maybe that's what they had then.

She sighed and moved on to the other cupboard, this one a jumble of huge seashells, pink, violet, bone-white. They looked, she thought, with their open ends toward her, as if they were all humming with the sound of the sea, which she knew she would hear if she opened the cupboard door, took one out and held it to her ear. She wondered if the humming of so many shells would fill the room if she *were* to open the door.

But she moved restlessly on, with an odd

feeling that she was looking for something, though she didn't know what. She peeked behind chairs and behind the large gold fan that seemed to have been pushed aside when the gas was lighted in the fireplace. She smoothed out the wrinkle in the rug behind it. She even looked under the cushions of the davenport. It was while she was straightening the last cushion that the glitter of one of the tiny teacups caught her eye.

"The doll!" she whispered. "I wish I could find the doll!" What if the doll was still in the house? What if she could find her? What if she explored the whole house, even—the word "attic" flashed into her mind and her thoughts went bounding up the stairs, to a mysterious place at the top of the house, a place Aunt Sarah had called dusty and dirty. But hadn't Aunt Sarah said something else about the attic, the night before, in her room, something about old things being stored in the attic—the old things in the picture?

Sally sat down again upon the little flowered stool.

Aunt Sarah said not to go up there, she told herself.

But she isn't here, she answered, and besides, she said I'd "better not." That isn't exactly the same, is it?

She'll be awfully mad if she comes back and finds me poking around up there. Sally was already standing up.

Well, I'll hurry and I won't hurt anything. I'll just look. This might be my only chance to go up there.

She could *feel* the huge dark attic yawning far, far above her, beneath the tall trees that shaded the house. And she shivered. Attics were full of black shadows and queer shapes, especially strange attics—and especially forbidden attics.

But she found herself at the bead curtains.

She pushed through them into the hall. Her knees were shaking, but she made herself go on, up the long stairway, touching the cold foot of the stone angel for good luck.

She had forgotten all about Shadow.

The Attic

SALLY DID NOT NOTICE, as she made her way up the winding staircase, that Shadow was following close behind. She was hurrying, sometimes taking two steps at a time, for she felt that there was no time to lose. Aunt Sarah might return at any moment.

As she stepped onto the carpet of red flowers in the upper hall, the grandfather clock at the other end of the hall gave the loud click which came before its chiming, as if the clock had to take a deep breath before beginning the hard work of telling the hour. Sally jumped nervously. "Shh," she whispered to the clock, but it went slowly on with its chiming. Standing there, looking down the long expanse of hall at the enormous clock, she felt as if it was speaking to her. "From now on," it seemed to be saying, "things will be different." The deep tones vibrated through her body, as if the upstairs had become the inside of a great clock. The very walls trembled. She felt trapped there, unable to move until the clock finished. Behind her, Shadow stopped to lick a paw. As the deep notes died away, and the melodeon shivered a tiny response from the parlor, she listened for a moment, and hearing nothing at all downstairs, she took a deep breath and began to step very quietly from flower to flower upon the carpet, as if they were stones in a stream she must cross. Shadow silently followed.

Of the many doors on either side of the hall, the only ones Sally was sure about were her own, second from the end on the left side, and the bathroom, right next to it. Which one of all the others could be the door to the attic?

Sally opened the first door she came to. From the shadowy room behind it her own face looked out at her, and she heard a whisper of movement. Her heart gave a great thump. The other Sally! she thought. But it was only her own reflection in a tall gold-framed mirror that stood in the center of the room. There was nothing else at all in the room. The sun, coming through the drawn shades at two windows, made yellow rectangles of light upon the bare wooden floor. It was the long curtains on the windows that had stirred at the opening of the door, and made the whispering sound that had frightened her. She drew a shaky breath and gently closed the door. She went on to the next room. In here she found a bed so high that a little pair of polished steps led up to it. A ruffled white canopy supported by slender posts seemed to be floating high above the bed. It was a bed such as she had seen before only in pictures, and it was very beautiful. A pale green rug of a soft furry material lay upon the polished floor, looking like the fur of some animal dreamed by whoever slept in that strange bed. A closet door stood slightly open, and stepping a little into the room, she peered into it. Something black was hanging there, swaying a little. The dress Aunt Sarah had worn yesterday! Then this was her room! The beautiful bed was her bed! Sally turned and ran the few steps to the door, and hurried out of the room, shutting the door behind her.

She opened the next door. A wooden stairway showed faintly in the light from the hall. It rose steeply up from the doorway and disappeared into the deeper darkness of what must be the attic. Sally could hear a tiny pattering sound somewhere up there. Her knees began to shake again, and she would have closed the door and scurried back downstairs had it not been for the doll. She might be up there, Sally told herself, she might. But what would she do if she *did* find her? Aunt Sarah would never let her keep her. But she'd think about that later. There wasn't much time. She could hear the grandfather clock ticking and ticking.

There was a light switch on the wall and she clicked it on as she started up the stairs. A dull watery light appeared above her, but the attic was still much too dark for comfort. Heart pounding, she continued up the stairs. She heard the pattering sound again and just then something soft brushed against her leg. She was so startled that she scarcely kept herself from falling. For one terrible moment she imagined that the green rug on Aunt Sarah's floor had followed her. She stood there in a panic, not knowing which way to go, and then she saw that it was not the rug at all but Shadow, who had run ahead of her up the stairs. She looked up the long stairway. She could see dust drifting in clouds, slow and dreamlike in the faint light up there, and further back, the deep blackness into which Shadow had disappeared. She swallowed the lump in her throat, and hesitated. She could hear Shadow moving around, bumping across the floor, and she was afraid of him, afraid of meeting his narrow green eyes staring at her from some dark corner—

But at that moment she heard the creak of the branches of the tall trees which grew over the house, and then again, the faint pattering. She looked up. The sound seemed to be coming from very high up, from the roof even. Why, she thought, that must be squirrels. They

must jump down from the trees and run across the roof.

She took a deep breath and continued on up the stairs. Despite the light from the single bulb, which she could scarcely see far up in the dusty rafters, it was very dark. The tiny windows high up on the walls were so covered with dirt and cobwebs that it seemed the sun must never get through them. Another tall mirror, leaning against an old chest of drawers, reflected a dusty picture of herself, looking quite lost and bewildered beneath the heavy cobwebs which hung like gray lace from the rafters. She could hear Shadow again, chasing something across the floor. Nothing else at all was moving in that great silent house. Sally began to walk around the attic, peering into corners, behind old bureaus and broken cupboards, and chairs and sofas with the stuffing leaking out.

Pushed back against the walls there were a number of old-fashioned trunks, some tall and thin, with fancy golden keys protruding from their fronts. They looked like enormous musical toys that would begin playing a solemn sort of music if the keys were turned. Others were squat, their rounded tops stripped with brass. Sally, attracted by a faint glimmer in one corner, approached it and found, hanging from a hook in the wall, a shimmering dress of silver sequins.

It swayed as if it were dancing, and she touched it gently, wondering who had worn it. Surely not Aunt Sarah. Like the melodeon and the bed, it was far too pretty.

And just then, oddly enough, a finger of sunlight managed to make its faltering way through a tiny space in one of the cobwebbed windows. It shuddered across the attic and fell on a trunk, lighting up a small brass rectangle attached to the front of its rounded lid. Sally walked closer to the trunk and peered down at it. Something was written on the little brass plate, scratched into it. She bent closer, and rubbed at the dust that coated it. "Sally," it said, in the finest, most delicate writing she had ever seen. It was just as if the trunk had spoken to her.

As if in a dream, she reached out and lifted the trunk's heavy lid.

The Diary

THE TRUNK OPENED WITH a faint, protesting screech. A puff of dust rose from its interior. Sally began to cough. She closed her eyes and waved her arms at the dust. When she opened her eyes, the dust had settled somewhat and she could see in the trunk, at the very top, the rather crumpled but still bright yellow bonnet that the other Sally was wearing in the painting. Trembling with excitement, she lifted the bonnet from the trunk and brushed at the fine dust that covered it. Carefully, she placed it upon her head. She found that it fitted her exactly. She ran over to the mirror, looked at herself and tied the ribbons in a bow beneath her chin. Yes, it was the very bonnet in the picture, and she *did* look just like the other Sally, except for the rest of my clothes, she thought, looking down at her short skirt and saddle shoes. She could see a corner of the open trunk behind her in the mirror, and remembering that there were other things in it, she hurried back and reached again into the trunk. This time she brought out the pale blue dress in the picture, and then a lace-edged petticoat and a pair of high-buttoned shoes. She was laughing out loud with delight by now, and Shadow had come to watch her. He sat in a pale patch of sunlight on the dusty floor, blinking in a superior sort of way each time she laughed, as if he were warning, "You won't be laughing for long." But Sally was far too excited to worry about him now.

However, she did look anxiously toward the stairs for a minute, and she listened before removing her own clothes and putting the others on. But all that she could hear in the rest of the house was the steady ticking of the grandfather clock.

She found the shoes rather hard to manage. The little round buttons kept slipping from her fingers, and at last she left a number of them undone. She wondered how the other Sally had made them work. Everything, even the shoes, fitted perfectly. She ran to the mirror and could hardly believe what she saw. She looked just like the other Sally in the picture. "I *am* the other Sally!" she whispered. She swayed back and forth, dreamily watching how the skirt swirled around her shoe tops. And as she swayed, she found that her hands were curving in front of her, as if they were holding something. The doll, she thought—that was the one part of the picture still missing.

The trunk! The doll had to be in the trunk! Oh, what if Aunt Sarah came back now! She ran frantically back to the trunk, leaned over its side, and reached again into its dark interior. Her hand closed upon something hard and slender, and she drew it out. She was holding the handle of a rolled silk parasol. She pressed the little button on the handle. Slowly the parasol creaked open, revealing layer after layer of pink ruffles. It was like watching a rosebud open. How pretty it looked, blooming there in the dark attic. Did the other Sally carry the parasol on sunny days? she wondered.

But she put it down almost immediately and took up the search for the doll, feeling that at any moment she might hear Aunt Sarah's footsteps downstairs.

This time she began throwing things helter-skelter from the trunk, shawls and muffs, dresses and gloves. She even found a doll, but the wrong doll entirely, a very nice doll with a china face and brown hair, but not at all the one she wanted. She felt like crying with disappointment as she laid her gently upon the growing pile of clothes on the attic floor.

At last there was nothing else at all in the trunk. She was ready to put everything back again when she noticed, way at the very bottom in a dark corner, a small book. She leaned over the side of the trunk, picked the book up, and brought it out. The covers of the book were of soft brown leather, and there were some letters stamped on it in gold. But because it was quite dark where she was sitting, she could not read them. She looked around the attic for a spot where there might be a little more light, and found that Shadow was still sitting in the small pool of thin sunlight that made its way through one of the dusty windows. Sally looked uncertainly at him, and then walked over and sat down next to him. She held the little book into the light. Stamped upon the cover was the word "Diary," and beneath it, "1899." Sally opened the soft cover and looked at the first page. "Sally" was written there. The yellowed old page seemed to be whispering her name in a graceful handwriting which had faded over the years to a very faint brown. Beneath the name was written, "Age eight."

Why, she was just my age, Sally thought, and she turned the brittle old page with trembling fingers. "January First" read the printing at the top of this page. The writing beneath it looked almost golden in the faint light. The words seemed to have been very carefully formed, and with their pretty loops and swirls they gave a lacy appearance to the page. Here and there the words had tumbled and spilled a bit over the faded blue lines of the paper. As she sat there on the attic floor, reading what the other Sally had written so long ago, Sally felt almost as if the other Sally were speaking to her, and that if she were, her voice would sound just the way the pretty golden handwriting looked. Perhaps, she thought, the other Sally had written this page with the feather pen on the desk in her room, sitting there on a day like this one, tickling her cheek with the tip of the feather and thinking . . .

But no, it wouldn't have been a day like this at all—it was New Year's Day, and maybe it was snowing . . .

"Dear Diary," the other Sally had begun, "I will write something every day. It snowed and snowed all day and yesterday too. Mama says we will be snowbound if it continues. I do hope so, for then I will not go to school. But I suppose I would take my lessons with Mama. It is cozy inside with Mama and Papa and little Bub. He is my baby brother and we call him Bub because he makes bubbling sounds with his mouth. Mrs. Perkins helps my mama to care for him. She is very funny, because she calls everyone, even kittens, dear little things. My aunt Tryphone lives here too and she is very old. Her father knew George Washington when he was President but I do wish she would not say it so much. I was

playing with my rag doll Elizabeth (so that was the doll's name, thought Sally—Elizabeth!) in my bedroom tonight and Mama came and said that she had a surprise in the kitchen. It was a wonderful surprise! My black cat, Mrs. Niminy Piminy, has three new kittens! Their eyes are not open yet. I gave one of them to Elizabeth and we played by the fire in the kitchen. Elizabeth's cat is named Tom and he is black like Mrs. Niminy Piminy. I think that Elizabeth and Tom will be good friends."

Sally turned the page very carefully because the paper was so brittle that she was afraid of tearing it. But to her disappointment the other Sally had not kept her promise to write every day in her diary at all. Sally turned page after page, hoping that there was more. But it was not until July 10 that she found another entry.

She settled back with a sigh of relief and began to read.

"Mama said that I must take care of Bub and Patience in the garden. Patience is a very little girl and I did not want to play with her and Bub cried a lot. But Mama said that I must, for Patience and her mama were coming to visit. Patience broke the handle of one of my little teacups (so that was how it got broken, thought Sally, remembering the little cup without a handle in the cupboard downstairs). I told her I didn't care but I really did. And then Elizabeth saved a little hoptoad's life! She fell over and she made me notice that Tom was trying to catch it, and the toad hopped right into my cup of tea and we laughed. Mama let me light the gas plant at night. I saw Tom holding Elizabeth in his mouth and I made him put her down. That naughty Tom! He thinks that Elizabeth belongs to him!"

Again, the entries stopped for a long time. It was not until December 24 that there was another. But the writing on this page had changed. It sloped down and had grown smaller and rather pinched-looking. Something was wrong, thought Sally, and she began to read.

"Papa took Mama and me in the sleigh to get our Christmas tree from the forest. It is very big. We put Elizabeth on top for a Christmas tree angel. She looked very beautiful. Mama played the melodeon and we all sang Christmas carols. When I looked around, Elizabeth was gone! We cannot find her anywhere. I miss her very much."

Sally thought that perhaps a teardrop had fallen on this page, for the ink was smudged toward the end.

She sighed deeply, thinking of what a sad Christmas Eve that must have been for the other Sally, but she turned the page, confident that Elizabeth would be found the next day. To her surprise, there were no more entries in the little diary. That was all.

"But what could have happened?" she wondered, looking up at the tiny bits of dust dancing in the shaft of sunlight.

"Did she find Elizabeth?" she asked, looking at Shadow. But Shadow only blinked his eyes and yawned.

They must have found her! She couldn't just disappear forever, could she? She must have fallen down among the branches of the tree, and the next day they found her.

But did they?

"I wish I knew for sure," she said.

She turned and looked at her reflection in the mirror.

"Where *is* Elizabeth?" she whispered to the girl in the mirror.

The Mirror

BUT THE GIRL IN the mirror did not answer, of course.

Sally stood there in the strange clothes, gazing at her reflected self in the dusty mirror and wondering how it had felt to be the other Sally.

I do look just like her, she thought.

She lifted her hand. The girl in the mirror lifted hers. She waggled her fingers at the mirror. The other girl did the same. She smiled. So did the girl in the mirror. She took off her bonnet. The mirror girl took hers off. They both placed the bonnet upon the floor, still smiling at each other.

They straightened and stood looking rather uncomfortably at each other, arms hanging at their sides, fingers twiddling a little.

"I wonder if you really did look so much like me," Sally whispered at last. "Did you feel like me? Were you ever sad or scared like me? I guess you were, when Elizabeth was lost, weren't you?" And it seemed to her that it might be the girl in the mirror who was asking her those very questions.

She sat down.

The girl in the mirror sat down.

Wouldn't it be funny, she thought, if that really was the other Sally in the mirror. "Do you think there's such a thing as magic?" she whispered to the other girl. The girl in the mirror seemed to be asking the same thing. Sally reached up and rubbed a clear space upon the dusty surface of the mirror, and of course, the other girl from her side of the mirror did the same thing.

Maybe, Sally thought, that really *was* the other Sally in there. She leaned closer to the mirror. "There," she whispered, "can you see me better? I can see you." Her breath had made a little circle of mist on the mirror. Or was it the other girl's breath, clouding it from the other side? You couldn't really tell for sure, Sally thought, feeling as if she'd made an enormous discovery. Did anyone know for sure? Maybe she was a reflection to her. Maybe the other Sally could see her too.

"Sally," called a voice, very close by.

Sally jumped and looked toward the attic stairs. Her heart turned over. It's Aunt Sarah! she thought. But there was no one in the attic but herself and Shadow, sleepily watching her from his patch of sunlight. The slow, drowsy dust was drifting, rising, falling. Shadow yawned.

The deep pink cavern of his mouth widened so that it seemed he might swallow the attic—trunks, cobwebs, Sally and all. She yawned too and rubbed her eyes. She felt very stiff and she stretched and yawned again. I must be imagining things, she told herself.

When she turned back to the mirror, she saw that the reflected girl was looking over her shoulder too, just as if she had heard the voice.

It was a moment before Sally realized how strange this was.

"But I'm not looking over my shoulder now," she said aloud. There was a cold, prickly feeling along the back of her neck. Tick, tick, tick, said the grandfather clock from the hallway below. Tick, tick, tick. How loud it was suddenly.

It was just then that the girl in the mirror spoke. "What is it, Mama?" she asked quite clearly, and with her profile still turned to the astonished Sally, she looked up and smiled.

Sally stretched a trembling hand out to the mirror. She placed her palm against it. She could feel only its cold, smooth surface.

But just as if she were not aware that she was only a reflection in a mirror, the other girl was now standing up. She reached a hand up, still smiling, and another hand reached down, clasped hers, and helped her to her feet.

Sally stood watching on the other side of

the mirror. This is the strangest thing that ever happened to me, she told herself. But even as she said it, something else happened. Quite suddenly, *she* was the girl in the mirror. It was *her* hand in the hand of the lady who stood smiling down at her, a lady who looked somehow like a much younger and far more pleasant Aunt Sarah!

"Come." said the other Sally's mother. Sally, who was now seeing everything from *inside* the mirror, realized that the lady also looked like her own mother, whose eyes sparkled in this same pleasant way when she smiled.

But she isn't really my mother, so I must be dreaming, Sally told herself. This can't be happening, because there's no way I can really be inside a mirror, is there? Even though it feels as if I am? There was no use asking the lady, who didn't seem to notice that anything unusual was going on. She thinks *I'm* the other Sally, thought Sally, only she doesn't know there *is* another Sally. I guess that if she did, *I'd* be the other Sally. This line of thought made her feel so dizzy that she closed her eyes and counted to ten. When she opened them, the lady was still there, holding her hand and smiling down at her. It felt like magic.

That was it! Something magic must be happening, and it was scary, but it was also very exciting. I'd better just calm down and see what happens next, Sally told herself. I might never get another chance like this.

"Let's go down to the kitchen," the lady was saying. "I have a surprise for you!"

"A surprise!" cried Sally. "What is it?"

"If I told you, it wouldn't be a surprise, would it?" answered the lady in a teasing voice. "Come along. Don't forget Elizabeth."

And Sally bent to pick the doll up from the floor where she had been lying all the time, just behind her.

Sally could see now that they were not in the attic at all, but in her bedroom. Now how could I have thought I was in the attic? she wondered as she followed her mother to the door, skipping a little as she went, and hugging dear old Elizabeth close to her. "How funny," she said, pausing at the door and looking back around the room. "What's funny?" asked her mother impatiently.

"Oh, I don't know, the room, I guess—the walls look so blue—" She yawned. "Excuse me," she said.

"Gracious!" said her mother, staring down at her. "Of course they're blue! They've been that way for years. Maybe the light at night makes them look a little different."

"Yes," said Sally. "The lights—they look

strange to me too—it's as if I never noticed them before—the little flames—the way they dance and sputter under the glass." She laughed and looked up at the familiar gas fixtures on the wall. "Isn't that funny?" she said. "They look so new to me, and my bowl and pitcher—do I really break the ice on my bowl in the morning before I wash my face? It seems like such a queer thing to do."

"Goodness gracious!" said her mother, placing a cool hand upon her forehead. "Are you feverish? No, just a bit warm." She glanced over at the fire crackling in the little green fireplace. "I expect you've been sitting too near the fire for too long."

"I guess I was dreaming," said Sally. "I think I must have fallen asleep by the fire just before you came in. Yes, I *was* dreaming—I remember now—I think I was dreaming that I was living in another time—but in this house—and I was scared. I think I was scared of a witch!" As she looked up at her mother, she could feel her lips trembling.

Her mother laughed and gently smoothed her hair. "My little dreamer," she sighed. "I hope you smiled your prettiest and made the witch disappear."

Sally shook her head. "I don't remember," she said.

"Well," said her mother briskly, "it's no wonder

you were sleeping. It's very late. You really ought to be in bed. Now come, please, no more nonsense if you want to see the surprise."

Sally gave a little hop of pure pleasure. The dream was almost forgotten. "Let's go now," she said. But just as they were leaving the room, the edge of one of the windows caught her eye. "Why, it's snowing!" she said.

"Oh my goodness, I do declare!" cried her mother, stopping and placing her hands on her hips, and looking down at her with a perplexed frown creasing her forehead. "Why, you're still half asleep." She sighed and brushed at the front of Sally's dress. "And your dress is all wrinkled. Of course it's snowing! You know very well it's been snowing for days and days. We're very nearly snowbound."

But Sally was still gazing in wonder at the fat swirling flakes of snow, which seemed to her to be exploding from the darkness beyond the window.

"I had a sort of summer feeling," she said.

"Well, I've told you not to stay so near that fire," scolded her mother. "Now come along before you fall asleep again!" And they went out of the room, across the flower-covered carpet of the upstairs hall, and off down the stairs, while the grandfather clock ticked and ticked. Sally's dream faded away to nothing as they went down and down. They passed the stone angel, holding aloft her little flaming lamp (Sally touched her cold foot and, as always, a pleasant shiver went through her as she did so, as if the angel, in some secret way, had spoken to her); they pushed through the bead curtains and on through the parlor, where the gaslights on the walls sputtered a pleasant little tune to the faint accompaniment of the melodeon, which whispered its usual greeting at their approach. In almost every room of the house a fire purred like a living thing. And all around, the snow was falling, softly and softly, upon the garden and upon the roof, and no doubt upon the little schoolhouse down the road and the church and the big red barn. It was piling up along the edges of the windows; and far off beyond the muffling snow, there was the faintest tinkle of sleigh bells. How cozy and pleasant it was in here, with the fire crackling in the fireplaces, throwing leaping shadows on the walls, and the little gas flames winking at her, and how lovely it was to be hurrying toward a surprise. "What do you suppose it is, Elizabeth?" she asked, hugging the little doll. But Elizabeth, if she knew, did not say.

"Will I like it?" she asked her mother.

"I think so," said her mother. "I rather think you will."

"Is it something to eat? Is it hot chocolate?"

But her mother only laughed and hurried her on through the dining room, her long skirts whispering over the floor as she moved. As they passed the round dining-room table, Sally caught a glimpse of herself reflected in its shining surface, and she wondered, with just the edge of her mind, what if the girl in there was a real girl, and she was just a reflection?

"What funny things I'm thinking tonight," she said to Elizabeth.

By then they were pushing through the door into the warm kitchen.

The front of the black iron woodstove glowed red. The comfortable smell of simmering soup swirled about the kitchen from the iron kettle at the back of the stove. A tremendous crackling and crashing of logs issued from the flaming throat of the stone fireplace. If the smaller fireplaces purred, this one roared. The ticking of the little church clock on the mantel could not even be heard.

Sally's father was kneeling on the hearth, his back to her. He was bending over something that she could not see.

"Where is the surprise?" she asked her mother eagerly. But her mother did not answer at once.

White-haired Aunt Tryphone sat in her rocking chair, her wrinkled old hands quiet upon the knitting in her lap, her gold-framed spectacles slipping down her nose. She was gazing down at the hearth, a smile playing about the corners of her mouth. Plump Mrs. Perkins was holding Sally's baby brother, Bub, in her arms. His pink fists were waving in the firelight, his eyes were closed tight and his mouth was screwed up and making the odd bubbling sounds for which he was famous. Mrs. Perkins was also looking at the hearth. "The little dears," she was saying in a happy, trembly sort of voice. "Just see the little dears."

"Here she is," announced Sally's mother as they approached the group around the fire. "I've brought Sally down to see."

"But where is the surprise?" Sally asked again, feeling as if she would burst into sparks like the fireplace logs if they did not tell her soon.

Sally's father turned his head and grinned at her over his curly black beard. Aunt Tryphone said in her shaky old voice, pointing a trembling finger at the hearth, "It's right there, just see, Sally dear."

Mrs. Perkins said, "The little dear tiny things."

"My dear papa once spoke with Mr. Washington," said Aunt Tryphone. "And even that blessed man never saw dearer, I can assure you."

Sally's father motioned to her and moved to let her in beside him. He pulled her close to him with a gentle hug and a kiss upon her ear.

And there, on the hearth, in a round basket, lay Sally's black cat Mrs. Niminy Piminy, curled comfortably around three very new kittens, whose eyes were tightly closed, but from whose tiny mouths came weak little mewing noises. Mrs. Niminy Piminy looked lazily up at Sally and blinked proudly. Her pink tongue darted out to lick the tiny round head of the orange kitten. The striped gray one rolled over on its back and mewed in astonishment, waving its stubby legs in the air.

"Oh!" cried Sally, and she dropped Elizabeth, who fell with her chin on the edge of the basket, so that she was staring directly into the face of a very, very tiny all-black kitten. One of her soft cotton hands rested gently on the kitten's small head.

"Oh, look," cried Sally, "Elizabeth's chosen that one. It will have to be hers! Oh, Mrs. Niminy Piminy, how beautiful, oh, how beautiful they are!" And she softly stroked the head of her dear old cat, who purred a deep, rolling purr that clearly expressed the utmost pride and satisfaction in her new family. The firelight danced on the happy flushed faces clustered in

what might have seemed to Mrs. Niminy Piminy a congratulatory garland around her basket. Sally leaned over and hugged Mrs. Niminy Piminy, and then she hugged her again.

The Doll

SALLY PETTED AND ADMIRED the kittens to her heart's content. Far above her the voices of the grown-ups murmured, Aunt Tryphone's rocking chair creaked, and it all mingled with the crackling of the fire, till it was hard to distinguish the various sounds from one another.

"Time to go to bed," said her mother suddenly, but when Sally begged, "Please, just a little longer," her mother sighed and got up to stir the soup on the stove. Clink, clink went the spoon against the iron kettle. Mrs. Perkins took Bub upstairs to bed. The back door opened and let in a great swoosh of cold air as Sally's father, after ruffling her hair with his big hand, went out to "see to the horses." A feather of snowflakes drifted in through the opened door, lifted, fell and melted in the warm kitchen before the flakes touched the floor. And after a time, the shadow of Aunt Tryphone's rocking chair lay quite still on the hearth, for Aunt Tryphone had fallen asleep over her knitting.

So it was that Sally, thoroughly happy, curled

up and fell asleep by the fire, one hand still resting on Mrs. Niminy Piminy's soft fur.

She stirred and sighed when she felt a hand upon her shoulder.

"Sally," whispered a voice that seemed to be coming from very far away. Then, "Sally," it said again, closer this time. She opened one eye and smiled sleepily.

She closed the eye again immediately, for it seemed to her that it was Aunt Sarah who was bending over her, shaking her shoulder.

"Come, Sally," said what was unmistakably the voice of Aunt Sarah. "You're awake now. Stand up."

Sally opened both eyes this time. Yes, it was indeed Aunt Sarah, looking very cross.

"Why, Mrs. Niminy Piminy," Sally said in surprise. For a black cat was curled up in the crook of her arm, purring quite happily. "You came with me." She rubbed her cheek gratefully against the cat's silky fur.

"Shadow seems to have taken a liking to you," said Aunt Sarah gruffly.

"Shadow!" cried Sally, and this time she sat up and stared down at Shadow, who blinked up at her in what seemed to be a surprisingly friendly manner. She smiled back at him rather timidly, and then hesitantly reached out and touched the top of his head gently with the tips of her fingers. Shadow purred and rubbed his head against the fingers.

"He likes to be petted under the chin too," said Aunt Sarah.

Sally gazed at Shadow, who looked very much as if he was waiting expectantly, and stroked him beneath the chin. Shadow lifted his throat luxuriously and poured out his contentment in a ripple of rising and falling purrs.

"I didn't think you liked cats, Sally," said Aunt Sarah.

Sally peeked up at Aunt Sarah and smiled shyly. "Oh, but I do," she said. And she wasn't afraid of Shadow anymore, she thought. He seemed so much like Mrs. Niminy Piminy.

But where was Mrs. Niminy Piminy? She looked into the mirror, but all that she saw was herself, and Shadow, and Aunt Sarah.

"Oh," she sighed, "it must have been a dream."

"You did look as if you were dreaming," said Aunt Sarah. "You looked happier than *I've* ever seen you. It must have been a good dream."

"Oh, it was," said Sally eagerly, "it was all about the other Sally, and Mrs. Niminy Piminy and the kittens."

Her aunt was staring down at her. Sally's heart jolted and she felt quite dizzy with anxiety. She remembered that her aunt had told her

not to come to the attic. Sally looked down at the clothes she was wearing. Aunt Sarah must be furious with her for putting them on! She probably thought she had torn them! She would punish her for taking all the things out of the trunk. Her eyes turned miserably to the untidy piles on the floor.

But her aunt, when she spoke, did not sound so much angry as puzzled. "Mrs. Niminy Piminy?" she said. "But how could you know? Oh I see!" she said as her eyes lit upon the little book that still lay open on the floor. "You read about her in the diary, I suppose. But come now, Sally, you've diddled and dawdled here quite long enough. It's past time for lunch, and you have all these things to put neatly away. I hope you know how to be neat? And just look at your clothes over there in a pile, all wrinkled and dirty. What would your mother say? Hurry now and take those things off."

Yes, thought Sally, getting unhappily to her feet, that sounded more like the Aunt Sarah she was used to. And yet, she didn't sound nearly so furious as Sally had feared. And somehow, she wasn't quite so afraid of her. I must be getting used to her, she thought. Besides, the happiness of her dream had stayed with her; yes, the *feeling* of her dream had come back with her, and she was finding it quite hard not to smile.

"Oh my!" cried Aunt Sarah as Sally rose to her feet and smoothed the long skirt.

Sally looked anxiously at her. What had she done now?

"Those clothes!" said Aunt Sarah. "Standing up like that, you look so much like—like the girl in the picture." Her voice faded to a trembling whisper.

Sally continued to look at her aunt. How old she was! She hadn't really noticed before that Aunt Sarah was really a very old lady. Perhaps not quite so old as Aunt Tryphone, but very old indeed.

After she had put everything back into the trunk, with her aunt's assistance, and was changing back into her own clothes, her aunt asked, "What made you come up here, Sally? It seems to me that I asked you not to," she added severely.

"I'm sorry," said Sally in a voice muffled by the blouse she was pulling over her head. "I was looking for Elizabeth."

"Did you say Elizabeth?" asked her aunt sharply as Sally's head appeared over the top of the blouse.

Sally nodded. "The doll in the picture," she said.

"Yes, I know," said her aunt impatiently, "but the doll was lost a long time ago."

Sally nodded. "I know. On Christmas Eve. I didn't know that when I came up, but I read about it in the diary." How funny, she thought, to be talking to Aunt Sarah like this, just as if she was anybody. "But I thought probably the other Sally found her after that."

"Well, you ought to have asked me," said her aunt. "I could have saved you a lot of trouble."

Sally stopped tying her shoe and looked up.

"Because," said her aunt, "the doll was never found."

"Never?" Sally's voice echoed her dismay around the attic. The very dust seemed to droop, lose spirit.

Her aunt shook her head from side to side. "Never," she said. "No one ever could find her again."

"Oh, that's terrible!" cried Sally. Tears misted her eyes, and she sniffed and brushed them away.

"Terrible? Why so terrible?" snapped her aunt.

"Because," said Sally, "the poor other Sally must have been so sad. She loved Elizabeth."

Her aunt did not say anything for a moment. Then, "Sad?" she said. "I expect she was. But she got over it. People do. They grow up."

"I wish—" said Sally.

"What?" asked her aunt.

"I don't know. I wish, I guess, that Elizabeth wasn't lost."

"No good wishing, Sally—too much wishing in the world. Not enough doing."

"But what could you do?"

"About what, for goodness' sake?"

"Why, about finding Elizabeth."

"Oh, I'm sure I don't know! All that's over and done with. Shadow!" called her aunt suddenly. "Come over here."

Sally could hear Shadow bumping around somewhere behind the trunks.

"There's a space between the floor and the ceiling," said her aunt, pointing, but Sally was not thinking about Shadow. "You see where the roof slopes down?" her aunt went on. "It doesn't quite meet the floor, and Shadow loves to push things down in there. What are you up to, naughty boy?" she asked fondly, looking down at him.

For Shadow had trotted obediently over to Aunt Sarah and was rubbing up against her leg.

As Sally followed her aunt down from the attic, she was thinking to herself that maybe it wasn't over and done with. Her dream had seemed so very real that she *couldn't* feel that it was all over. And if Elizabeth had been lost in this very house, then why shouldn't she be found in this very house? Maybe *I* can find her, she thought.

At least, she was going to try. But where, she wondered, did you begin?

Mystery

"WHAT ARE YOU LOOKING AT?" asked Aunt Sarah as they were eating tuna fish sandwiches at the kitchen table.

Sally swallowed a bite of her sandwich and said, "The kitchen—it looks different."

"Different? Different from what?"

"Well, different from my dream," she said.

"Dreams, dreams," said Aunt Sarah, but she did not sound unkind. "Well, tell me, how was it different?"

"There was a fire in the fireplace," said Sally.

"Hasn't been a fire there for years," said Aunt Sarah.

"And they were all sitting around it. Aunt Tryphone and the other Sally's mother and her father, and Mrs. Perkins and little Bub. He was awfully cute."

"Little Bub," said Aunt Sarah. "Yes, I suppose he was—cute, as you put it. How children do talk nowadays!"

But Sally scarcely heard her. "Why, it's a mystery!" she was saying. "There's a real mystery in this house!"

"What's a mystery?" asked Aunt Sarah.

"About Elizabeth."

Aunt Sarah sighed. "Still thinking about the doll, are you?"

Sally nodded. "It really *is* a mystery, because how could she get lost, with everyone there in the room? How could she disappear from the top of the Christmas tree? Where could she go?"

"Calm down, Sally, don't talk with your mouth full." Aunt Sarah sighed again. "I'm sure I don't know. She simply disappeared. That's all. No one's even thought about it for years and years till you came along."

"But it seems so funny!" Sally insisted, almost forgetting that she was talking to Aunt Sarah, for she felt as if she were thinking out loud. "Where could she have gone? Dolls can't walk."

To her astonishment, Aunt Sarah smiled. A very small and rather bleak smile it was, with somewhat the effect of sun breaking through winter clouds. "The other Sally, as you call her," she said, "used to think that Elizabeth was a little bit magic. But what nonsense I'm talking! All I can say is that no one ever solved the mystery in all these years. And that's what it's going to stay, if you want to call it that—a mystery."

"Could she have been caught in the branches? Yes, that's it! Maybe she fell, and when they threw the tree out—oh, but that would mean she really *was* gone—"

"I expect they thought of that," said Aunt Sarah. "Yes, they searched that tree needle by needle before it was burned, or probably they did."

"Then you really think they did?" cried Sally. "Then maybe she *is* here!—but how do you know?" she asked.

"You know things in a family," said Aunt Sarah, standing up and beginning to clear the table.

Sally, without thinking, began to help her as she did her mother at home, scraping and stacking the dishes upon the sink counter.

"Well," said Aunt Sarah, "I didn't think modern children knew how to do things so nicely. Perhaps you are going to be of some help to me after all."

Sally guessed that this was the closest Aunt Sarah ever came to a real compliment, and despite the odd way in which it was put, she felt pleased. "Shall I dry the dishes?" she asked.

"You'll find a towel in that drawer over there."

Sally opened the drawer. Inside she found a neat pile of folded dish towels, and a very old-looking gingerbread-boy cookie cutter.

She lifted it out and looked at it.

"That's a very old cookie cutter," said her aunt.

"Yes," said Sally. "Sometimes my mother lets me help make gingerbread boys at home. We have a cutter too. But not so big, or so old."

"Does she?" said Aunt Sarah, turning on the faucet. "You make gingerbread boys together, do you? You like that, I suppose?"

Sally nodded and dropped the cutter back into the drawer. She took out a towel and began to dry the dishes.

Neither of them spoke until the dishes were all done and put away.

Sally was thinking, however. Thinking about Elizabeth. Thinking about the attic. Maybe there was a clue up there. Maybe if she looked very carefully, she could find *something*.

Summoning up all her bravery, she asked at last in a rather faltering voice, "I wonder—if I could go back to the attic?"

Her aunt turned from the cupboard into which she was placing the last of the dishes. She looked at her. "Still dreaming about Elizabeth, are you? Well, perhaps tomorrow. We'll see. Right now, I think you'd better go outside and get some fresh air and sunshine. You can take Shadow out with you, now that the two of you are such friends."

Well, thought Sally, as she turned and walked toward the back door, it was better than nothing. Aunt Sarah had said "perhaps." But it was going to be awfully hard waiting for tomorrow. Her throat was feeling a little sore, but she wasn't going to mention it.

"Oh, and Sally," called her aunt as she and Shadow were going down the back steps of the porch to the tangled old garden, "I thought perhaps tomorrow we could, if you like, make some gingerbread cookies." But before Sally could reply, her aunt had closed the door and disappeared.

A Friend

"AUNT SARAH'S FUNNY, ISN'T SHE?" Sally whispered to Shadow. But Shadow was busily cleaning his left ear with a paw and did not bother to reply.

"Was this ever a real garden?" Sally wondered as they began to walk together through the tall weeds and grass. The breeze lifted her hair just as she had imagined it would. The soft fur of the foxtails tickled her knees, and Shadow sneezed as if perhaps it tickled his nose. She could see his tail moving through the grass, even when she lost sight of the rest of him.

The whisper of the moving grass rose all around them. Sally remembered how it had looked to her from her window. Like a green sea. She found that it was indeed a little like walking through water to make her way through the swaying grass. It flowed smoothly past her and resisted the movement of her legs just as she remembered the water doing at the lake where she sometimes stayed in the summertime.

She closed her eyes and imagined that she

was standing knee-deep in water. In a moment her mother would call to her from the shore. When she opened her eyes, she saw a glitter of white showing through the thrashing grass at her feet. She bent to pick it up. She straightened and looked at the bit of seashell curling up from the palm of her hand. For a moment it hardly seemed strange at all to find a shell out here. It looked like a broken piece of one of the shells in the parlor cupboard.

She put the bit of shell in her pocket, wondering how it had come to be out here. She walked on, looking at the ground for other shells, and attempting at the same time to avoid the tangled bushes that tore at her hair and her clothes. She began to notice, through the reaching branches, the fallen underbrush and overgrown weeds, faint ghosts of paths that once must have led about the garden.

"The other Sally must have walked here just like this, Shadow," she said, "with Mrs. Niminy Piminy. She was a black cat just like you, only she was a lady, of course, and she lived in this very house. Shadow, where are you?"

For the cat had entirely disappeared from view. Now how could he have done that? she wondered. She hadn't even seen him go.

"Here, Shadow," she called. "Here, kitty, kitty, kitty." But there was no sign of Shadow that she could see, anywhere in the garden. The branches of the apple trees stirred, spilling sun bangles through their leaves. Sally watched them tremble on the very tips of the swaying grass, and then blow away to touch lightly on others. For a moment the entire garden shimmered. The pine trees, shaded by the building at the back of the garden, looked very solemn, dipping their dark tops to her as if they were bowing.

The sun felt pleasantly warm on Sally's head. No one at all seemed to be moving in the apartment houses on either side of the garden. (How strange *they* would have looked to the other Sally.) She looked up at the windows and remembered how the windows of these very buildings had seemed to stare at her only last night. Now they did not look frightening at all. Only empty, as if no one lived behind them. There was no movement, nor any sound either, from Aunt Sarah's house. Only up at the open windows of her own bedroom, the yellow curtains fluttered in the breeze.

How still it was. She might have been the only person awake in the whole world. The whispering of the grass sounded to Sally like the voices of the children who had played here long ago—the other Sally, and Patience, and little Bub. How nice it would be to have someone to play with! Shadow wasn't really very satisfactory, even when he was around. She missed her friends at home.

Snap! The sudden noise made her jump. She looked up at the high wall of the apartment building beneath which she was standing. Just above her head, the cord of a window shade was swaying back and forth, as if the shade had snapped up suddenly. To Sally's surprise, she saw beneath the shade, and just showing over the edge of the windowsill, a red ribbon tied in a neat bow. The bow was trembling. As Sally watched, the bow slowly rose and was followed by a bright yellow head, which was followed in turn by a pair of round blue eyes, a turned-up nose, and a curly mouth rather like Elizabeth's, which seemed to be trying very hard not to tremble.

The girl, for it was a girl, leaned out of the window and looked down at her. Two very long yellow braids slipped forward and hung out of the window against the brick wall. The girl raised her hand and took a bite from a cookie. She continued to stare solemnly down at Sally.

Sally stared back, too surprised to say anything.

"Do you want a cookie?" whispered the girl.

"Yes," said Sally, and found that she was whispering too.

The girl vanished again beneath the window-sill, and shortly reappeared with another cookie in her hand. Leaning farther out of the window, she stretched an arm down to Sally. Sally stood up on her toes, braced herself against the building with one hand and with the other reached up and took the cookie from the girl. The end of one of the dangling braids tickled Sally's cheek. Her hand brushed against the vines which were growing up the side of the building from Aunt Sarah's garden.

"Thank you," she said. She looked at the cookie. It was a round one with crinkled edges and pink frosting. She took a bite. "It's good,"

she said, swallowing and smiling up at the girl.

"My mother made them," the girl said.

"It's very good. Your mother must be a good cook." She ate some more of the cookie.

"Yes, she is."

They stared at each other while they ate their cookies.

"Would you like another?" offered the girl.

Sally shook her head. "No, thank you," she said. "I just finished lunch."

A silence fell between them.

They both looked up while a bird sang briefly from the top of an apple tree.

"What's your name?" Sally asked at last, shading her eyes against the sun and peering at the girl.

"Emily."

"Mine's Sally. Can you come out and play?"

At this, the girl shook her head. Her braids thumped against the brick wall. The end of her pink tongue crept out and nervously touched her upper lip.

"Do you live here?" asked Sally, feeling disappointed. Still, perhaps they could talk for a while.

The girl nodded. "Do you live there?" she asked, pointing at the house with her half-eaten cookie.

"No," said Sally, "I'm just visiting my aunt Sarah."

"Oh," said Emily. Her tongue darted out again. She leaned forward a little and lowered her voice so that Sally had to move even closer to hear her. "There was no one living in that house for a long, long time." Her eyes grew very round and her mouth trembled as she stared at the house. "It was all closed up. It was dark!" To Sally's surprise, Emily shivered.

"I know," said Sally, wondering what was wrong with Emily. "I'm eight years old. How old are you?"

"Seven," said Emily. "Seven and a half." She was not looking at Sally.

Sally followed the direction of her gaze. Emily was looking up at the yellow curtains billowing at her windows.

"That's my room up there," said Sally, pointing. "I have a little green fireplace. It's very old."

Emily drew back from the window. Her braids slipped back inside over the sill. "Good-bye," she whispered. Her hand reached up for the cord of the shade.

"Oh, don't go!" cried Sally. "Please don't go. I was just wishing for someone to talk to."

Emily slowly lowered her hand. Her lips moved as if she were about to speak, but she did not say anything. Her eyes flicked toward Aunt

Sarah's house, and then turned away.

Sally looked up at her, feeling puzzled. Why, she's afraid! she thought. Just like I was! Maybe the house had looked haunted to her all this time, with all those scraggly old bushes, and that loose shutter creaking, and nobody living in it. And then Aunt Sarah had come— maybe she was afraid of Aunt Sarah!

"Guess what?" said Sally. "I came here last night in all that rain, and it was very dark, and I was so afraid! I never saw this house before, or my aunt Sarah either, and the house looked so spooky to me that I wanted to run away." She smiled.

"You did?" Emily said. "Really?" The tip of one braid appeared over the sill. "Aren't you afraid anymore?"

"No," said Sally. "Didn't you ever think it looked scary here?"

Emily nodded her head vigorously up and down.

"Why, I was even afraid of my aunt! I even thought maybe she was a witch."

Emily stared down at her own hands, which looked quite frozen on the windowsill. She took a deep breath. "That lady," she said. "I saw her when she moved in, with a black cat. She looked all bent over!"

"But she isn't a witch at all," Sally went on.

"She's just very old. I guess she's not used to children. Imagine thinking she was a witch! Wasn't that funny?" She laughed. "Why, tomorrow we're even going to make some gingerbread cookies."

A smile began very slowly upon Emily's face. The curly corners of her mouth curled even more, and then she gave what sounded like a very relieved giggle. The other braid appeared over the edge of the window. "I like gingerbread cookies," she said.

"You know," said Sally, "the house isn't really scary at all, once you get used to it. It's just very old, like Aunt Sarah. It's awfully pretty inside. There's a melodeon—that's a little thing like a piano—and it plays a tune all by itself when you just walk through the room, even if you go on tiptoe. And besides that"—she paused dramatically and looked up at Emily, who was giving her all her attention—"there's a very old doll lost somewhere in the house. There's a picture of her on the wall of my room. She belonged to a girl who lived here a long time ago. No one's ever found her."

Emily's eyes seemed to grow larger and become an even deeper blue.

"I'm trying to find her," said Sally.

Emily grinned. She seemed a quite different sort of girl now, one it would be a great deal of fun to know.

"I'll ask my mother if I can come out and play," she said. And then she was gone. The last Sally saw of her for a time was the glittering tip of one flying braid. Then the window was empty, except for the half-drawn shade and its dangling cord, moving slowly back and forth like a pendulum, ticking away the minutes while Sally waited. She picked up a twig from the ground and stroked the fur of a foxtail with it. A small green apple fell with a soft plopping sound and rolled away in the deep grass.

Then Emily was back again. Her face beamed her eagerness. "My mother says I can come over for a little while," she said. "I'll come around the front and through the alley." She pointed.

Sally was making her way through the tangle of bushes at the side of the house next to Emily's apartment house when Emily herself burst through from the other side. She was wearing a pinafore covered with small yellow quarter moons that repeated the smile of her own curly mouth. "Hi!" she said.

"Hi!" said Sally. They pushed through the bushes in the garden.

"What should we do?" Emily asked breathlessly.

Sally looked around the garden. Her eye lit upon the old barn, with the interesting glimmer

of red that she had seen from her window showing in the crack between the doors.

"Would you like to go into the barn?" she
asked.

Emily looked at the barn and then at Sally.
She nodded.

"What's that red in there?" she asked.

"I don't know. I've never been in there
either."

They walked through the blowing foxtails
to the barn. "They tickle my legs," said Emily. "I
know," said Sally. They giggled, just because
it was so wonderful to feel like old friends
already.

Reaching the barn, Sally pushed at the doors.
The old doors squeaked and groaned as if they
had not been subjected to such treatment in
many years. The space between them widened
enough to permit the two girls to slip through
into the barn. At the first squeak Emily's hand
had slipped into Sally's, and so hand in hand,
Emily a little behind, they entered.

Sally blinked at the darkness inside. She
could feel Emily's breath on the back of her
neck, and she squeezed her hand, feeling a
little frightened herself. The dirt floor was
spongy beneath her feet. She could feel its coldness through the soles of her shoes. The barn
smelled, as barns ought to, of dampness and

long-ago hay, and perhaps even of the horses who had once stood in the stalls. Sally imagined them turning their heads as the other Sally entered. Maybe she had carried sugar in her pocket for them, or an apple from the garden.

Emily gave a little shuddering gasp behind her.

"It's Shadow!" cried Sally. For there he was, sitting quite placidly on the high seat at the front of an enormous red sleigh. The runners of the sleigh rose in magnificent curves from the barn floor. "The sleigh in the diary!" Sally said.

The sleigh was standing between the two lines of stalls, illuminated from above, as if on a stage, by wavering ribbons of light that descended from holes in the roof of the barn. The sleigh itself was delicately frosted over with dust and silvery cobwebs. It looked enchanted to Sally, for it seemed to shine with a light of its own. A little silver step at the side of the sleigh winked invitingly.

Sally looked down at Emily, who was now standing at her side, staring up in wonder at the beautiful sleigh. Her tongue darted out and touched her upper lip.

"Don't be afraid," said Sally. Emily certainly seemed to be a very timid little girl, she thought. "It's only Shadow up there. He's a very nice cat."

"I'm not afraid," Emily said. "I'm not afraid with you, Sally. It's pretty. It's a very pretty sleigh," she added gravely.

"Let's get up into it," said Sally, feeling very brave.

"All right," agreed Emily.

"I'll go first," Sally offered.

She placed one foot on the silver step, and holding on to a projecting edge of the sleigh, lifted the rest of herself up to the step and then to the floor of the sleigh. The sleigh gave a profound sigh as she stepped into it, as if it, like the barn doors, had not been disturbed in years. Sally reached down and took Emily's hand and helped her up. Tiny cobwebs snapped soundlessly as they moved. The black leather seat was covered with a network of tiny cracks, so that it looked like a map of some heretofore undiscovered land. A fat white spider, who had perhaps been sleeping up there, scuttled away along one of the cracks and disappeared over the side of the seat. They sat down on the splitting seat and looked up at Shadow, who blinked down at them from the driver's seat, his green eyes glowing.

"Come on down, Shadow," Sally said. "I want you to meet Emily." Just as if he had understood, Shadow jumped down and sat between the two girls, rubbing against their sides in a friendly manner and purring. Sally stroked his fur. Emily hesitated only a moment before doing the same. Sally introduced Emily to him and Emily took his paw and said gravely, "How do you do, Mr. Shadow." Shadow purred his reply. Emily brushed her cheek against his head. "He's nice," she said.

Sally nodded. "I used to be afraid of him," she said, as if that had been a very long time ago. And indeed, it did seem to be. She told Emily about the diary, and about the other Sally and her cats. "This must be the very sleigh she rode in," she said, "on Christmas Eve. And I'll bet that she had Elizabeth with her."

"Who's Elizabeth?" asked Emily.

"The doll. The doll I'm going to find."

"I hope you do," said Emily. "But how will you find her?"

"I guess I'll just have to think very hard. And I'm going to look all through the attic for a clue if Aunt Sarah lets me go back up there. You see, Elizabeth was on the top of a Christmas tree, and they were all singing, and when they looked again, Elizabeth was gone. And there was no one else in the room at all. It's very mysterious."

"It's a real mystery," agreed Emily. "Maybe the cats saw what happened to her."

They laughed. "Do you think they did,

Shadow?" Sally asked. "Did Mrs. Niminy Piminy see what happened?"

As if in reply, Shadow pricked up his ears and then leaped gracefully down from the sleigh to the barn floor. He sat looking up at them, one ear cocked as if he were listening to something.

"Sally!" a voice called. Shadow looked once at the two girls and then hurried to the barn doors.

"Here I am," Sally called. Just as Shadow reached the doors, the crooked fingers of Aunt Sarah's hand appeared at the edge of one of them. Emily gave a small frightened cry. Aunt Sarah's face showed in the space between the doors. She blinked, shaded her eyes with her hand, and peered up at them. "Oh, there you are," she said, frowning into the darkness.

Oh dear, Sally thought, she would frighten Emily. "It's only Aunt Sarah, Emily," she whispered.

"Who's that with you?" asked Aunt Sarah.

"This is my friend Emily," Sally answered.

"Hello," Emily whispered.

"Hello, Emily," said Aunt Sarah briskly. "You girls can play later. Hurry now, Sally. It's your mother on the phone. You may be going home tomorrow. Don't make her wait. Hurry!"

"My mother!" Sally cried. She looked at

Emily. "Please wait," she said, and jumped down from the sleigh.

Emily nodded. Her hands were clasped tightly together in her lap.

A Decision

SALLY'S HAND WAS TREMBLING as she picked up the telephone receiver. "Hello, Mama," she said.

And from somewhere far away came a voice which scarcely sounded like her mother at all.

"Sal!" said the voice. "Oh, it's good to hear you! Are you all right, darling? Aunt Sarah says you have a little cold."

"Yes," said Sally, "I'm all right." Shadow had jumped up onto the telephone table and was watching her, his tail hanging off the table, the tip of it twitching back and forth. Aunt Sarah was standing somewhere nearby, behind Sally.

"You sound a little hoarse, Sal. Are you sure you're all right?" Sally cleared her throat. "I'm all right," she said. "I just ran in from the barn."

"Hi, Sal!" said her father's deeper voice.

"Hi, Dad," she said. "It's good to talk to you."

"Want your mom to come and get you, old girl?" he asked.

"Yes, Sal," said her mother, before she could answer, "I've really had enough sun, and your father can handle his business without me. What do you say, dear? When I gave Mrs. Chipley Aunt Sarah's address, I hardly expected—Aunt Sarah says she'd like to have you stay, but it's up to you."

"She—she does?" asked Sally.

"Yes, hon, that's what she said, but," and her mother lowered her voice, "I know that she's very old, dear, and not used to children, and maybe you feel—strange there? And I do miss you."

"I miss you too," said Sally, and then, to her surprise, she heard herself say, "but I'd like to stay here. I really would."

Aunt Sarah gave a little cough and cleared her throat.

"Are you sure, Sal?" asked her mother. "Very sure?"

"Yes, I'm sure. I like it here. I'm looking for a doll."

"A doll?"

"Yes, an old doll. She was lost here a long time ago, and maybe I can find her. I want to try."

"Well, my goodness, you do sound as if you're enjoying yourself. Are you very sure, Sal?"

"Sal," said her father, "we talked with Mrs. Chipley and she may not be able to get back before we do, though her daughter's getting along fine. We'll be back sometime before

school starts, but Mom's ready to leave now if you say the word."

"No, I really want to stay," said Sally. "Honestly, I do want to." For how *could* she go, with the mystery still unsolved?

"Shadow's licking my hand," she said, laughing. "It tickles, no, it scrapes, just like sandpaper. He's this black cat that Aunt Sarah has, and there used to be another black cat here named Mrs. Niminy Piminy. Isn't that a funny name? And there's an old red sleigh in the barn, and there was a girl who lived here a long time ago and she looked just like me, and her picture is hanging over a little green fireplace in my room, and I've found a friend. Her name's Emily."

Her mother was laughing. "Goodness!" she said. "It sounds quite exciting! I guess you really do want to stay. Very well, then, dear, but I'll give you our phone number here and you can call me the minute you change your mind."

"All right," said Sally, "but I don't think I will." She picked up a pencil, pushing Shadow off the pad of paper on the table, and wrote down the number her mother gave her.

"Good-bye, Sal," said her mother. "Watch that cold!"

"Good-bye, Punkin," said her father.

She hung up and turned to Aunt Sarah. To

her immense surprise, Aunt Sarah was smiling—and in a way that lit up her eyes so that she looked even more like the other Sally's mother, though her hair was indeed very gray.

Sally smiled shyly back at her.

But at this, Aunt Sarah turned her head to look at Shadow, cleared her throat, and said, "Well, Shadow's looking very happy that you're staying."

And so am I, thought Sally, catching a glimpse of herself in the mirror on the wall over the telephone. She gave a little skip that clearly expressed her pleasure as she followed Aunt Sarah from the hall.

She hurried back out to the garden and into the barn. "Emily," she called, before she had even gotten through the doors, "I'm staying! We can do all sorts of things!"

But the sleigh was quite empty. "Emily?" she called.

Her friend had vanished. As Sally stood there forlornly looking up at the sleigh, a cloud passed over the sun, and the ribbons of light were abruptly withdrawn. "Why did you go, Emily?" she whispered. "Aunt Sarah scared you away."

She went back into the garden and called. She stood beneath Emily's window and called. But there was no answer. The shade had been drawn down over the window again. Just as if she had been a little garden spirit, Emily had disappeared.

Somehow, it didn't seem so good to be staying here after all. Maybe she should have asked her mother to come. Maybe she should call her back.

But there was still Elizabeth.

Yes, I want to find Elizabeth, she told herself. And I will, somehow.

A Somewhat Festive Meal

DINNER THAT EVENING WAS a rather festive occasion, eaten at the big round dining-room table.

"A celebration," said Aunt Sarah as she lit the tall white candles she had placed on the table.

"What are we celebrating?" asked Sally, who was still feeling unhappy about Emily.

"Perhaps we're celebrating your visit here," said Aunt Sarah. "We haven't really done it properly yet, you know. I think Shadow is very happy to have you in the house. He's never had a child around, you see. That's why he was so unfriendly at first, I suppose. I believe he's sorry. I think he feels it's a happier house with you here."

Sally looked down at Shadow, who was sitting on the floor next to her chair, looking expectantly up at her. "Poor Shadow, he looks hungry," she said. Her hand hovered over the meat on her plate. "May I?" she asked, looking at her aunt through the wavering light of the candles.

"Oh, Sally," said her aunt sharply, "we

don't—" But then Aunt Sarah stopped, her face softened, and a smile started somewhere around her eyes, though it was hard to tell for sure by candlelight. "I think you may," she said. "I think Shadow would like that."

"Thank you," said Sally, and gave Shadow a piece of her meat. He flicked a grateful look at her as he took it.

How funny Aunt Sarah was, always talking about Shadow and how he felt. Did she mean *she* was happy to have Sally here too? Sally looked across the table at her. Aunt Sarah was touching her napkin to her lips and looking quite stern again. No, she probably was just glad that Shadow was happy. That was all she had said, after all.

Neither of them said anything for a time until Sally said, "I wonder if it looked like this when the other Sally lived here?"

"I imagine it did," said Aunt Sarah. "The other Sally did her homework at this very table. At least, I suppose she did." Aunt Sarah was standing up as she spoke. She looked very tall. Her movement disturbed the candle flames, and they wavered and then grew taller for a moment, lighting up Aunt Sarah's face from beneath and giving her a rather forbidding look. With a lurching of her stomach, Sally remembered how Aunt Sarah had looked like a witch to her at first.

But she didn't anymore, she thought. Aunt Sarah still looked stern, but not like a witch. All Sally's old fears seemed to have vanished that afternoon in the garden. Yes, she guessed she was getting used to her aunt.

"We're getting quite used to having you around," said Aunt Sarah, as if she had read Sally's mind. She began to clear the table. Sally jumped to her feet to help her. It was rather fun, handling the old blue-and-white dishes and wondering if the other Sally had perhaps carried these same dishes from this very table.

After a dessert of chocolate cake and pink ice cream, Sally removed the tablecloth while Aunt Sarah began washing the dishes in the kitchen. Sally was folding the cloth when she noticed that pressed into the polished wood of the tabletop were what seemed to be letters. She looked closer. An *S*, an *A*. She remembered what Aunt Sarah had said about the other Sally doing her homework here. I bet she forgot to put something under her paper, Sally thought. Now she could see an *L*, another *L*, and a *Y*. "Sally!" she whispered. She touched the letters with the tips of her fingers and for a moment felt very close to that other Sally. It was as if the years that had gone by did not matter at all.

By the time they had finished the dishes, Sally was feeling very tired. Her aunt remarked that it had been a long day and suggested that Sally go right off to bed.

She did so gratefully. When she had gotten into bed, Aunt Sarah looked down at her and said, "Well, good night, Sally," and left the room.

My mother always kisses me good night, thought Sally, but she did not say it. She lay there in the dark, missing her mother, and wondering at all the things that had happened that day.

She had not dared to ask again about going to the attic, and she was not at all sure that Aunt Sarah would let her. "Oh, I hope she will," she whispered to the darkness. "I hope she will."

The faces of the other Sally and Elizabeth in the picture above the fireplace showed in the moonlight more than the darker areas of the painting. Sally felt that the two of them were watching over her as she fell asleep.

A Summer Garden

IT WAS A DREARY MORNING she woke to. Rain was pouring down in earnest, drumming upon the roof, dripping from the treetops and gurgling in the gutters in a most depressing and dismal way. The entire house creaked as if it were a ship in a stormy sea.

Sally wondered as she woke why she was feeling so unhappy. Then she remembered—Emily—Emily had been scared away. Her only real friend in this whole place was gone forever. She sighed deeply and shifted her feet. Her throat was hurting again.

Shadow's head appeared suddenly over the humped-up blankets. His ears were back and his eyes were narrowed. He looked very cranky.

"Sorry, Shadow," she said wearily, "but you've been sleeping on my feet all night, and they're stiff."

Shadow grumbled something and lowered his head, curling up again at her feet, as if he too found it hard to face the day.

And as for Elizabeth, thought Sally, what

makes me think that after all these years I can find her?

She lay there, staring gloomily up at the picture of the other Sally, who seemed to be looking sad too, until Aunt Sarah called to her from the bottom of the stairs that breakfast was ready.

Down in the kitchen, Aunt Sarah was standing at the stove, stirring an enormous kettle of what seemed to be porridge. Sally could hear the bubbles bursting as they rose to the top of the kettle. It seemed to her that there was not a sadder, grayer sound in the world than the sluggish bursting of porridge bubbles.

I hate porridge, thought Sally, sitting down dispiritedly at the table and staring out at the gray rain.

Aunt Sarah's back was to her, and she was standing, one hand pressed against her back, in a bent-over position, just as she had been when Sally first saw her in the doorway, in the rain. A long strand of hair had escaped from the bun at the back of her neck, and was dangling over her shoulder. Sally looked at it and thought that she'd like to tuck it back where it belonged.

Aunt Sarah groaned. "Arthritis," she said. "Always bothers me when it rains. Getting old."

"I'm sorry," said Sally.

"Sorry!" snapped Aunt Sarah, turning around to glare at her. "Sorry doesn't set the table!" She turned back to the stove and began to stir the porridge furiously.

Sally, feeling hurt, got up and began to take dishes from the cupboard to set the table. She was feeling extremely sorry for herself. Even the merry ticking of the little church clock could not raise her spirits.

"You can get some prune juice from the refrigerator and pour it out," said Aunt Sarah.

Prune juice! thought Sally. If that wasn't just like this day! A prune-juice-and-porridge day exactly!

They sat down and ate their dismal meal in silence. Sally decided that after breakfast she'd call her mother. Yes, that's just what she would do.

"I'm sorry, Sally," said her aunt.

Sally looked up in surprise to see that Aunt Sarah was gazing anxiously at her.

"That's all right," Sally said, looking down at the grayish remains of her porridge floating sluggishly in the thin blue milk. "Drip, drip," whispered the rain.

Her aunt sighed. "It's a dreary day," she said, staring bleakly out the window. "And I got up feeling just miserable. I'm afraid I took it out on you."

"I felt awful too when I got up," Sally confessed. "All sort of gray."

"Well, you're not as gray as I am, at any rate," said Aunt Sarah, indicating her own hair.

Sally looked uncertainly at her aunt. But when Aunt Sarah gave a surprising snort that was a sort of laugh, Sally began to smile, and then she laughed too.

This really was a queer day, Sally thought. She never expected she'd be laughing with Aunt Sarah.

They did the dishes together in better spirits. "Why, Sally, I believe you've made my arthritis better already," said Aunt Sarah. Then she said, "How would you like to spend a rainy morning playing in the attic?"

Sally grinned at her aunt. "Oh, could I?" she cried.

"Run along," said her aunt. "Run along."

And off Sally went to the attic with Shadow following after her. He seemed quite revived by his breakfast, which he had eaten beneath the sink.

This time she made a systematic search of the attic. First, the trunk. But there was nothing there she hadn't seen before. Then she looked in other trunks, and in drawers and boxes. She turned up all sorts of finery, glittering beads and earrings, feather fans, old lace, ancient dresses with pearls or jet beads stitched into flower and butterfly patterns on their skirts. There were, besides, a man's high silk hat, a black satin shawl with a lining of rainbow silk, old paper-lace valentines, Christmas cards, yellowed letters tied into bundles with faded bits of ribbon, broken and battered Christmas tree ornaments, and a plush rabbit lacking one pink eye. At last, she was so tired that she simply sat down wearily on the floor and closed her eyes. Shadow was playing his usual game of pushing things into the space between the roof and the floor. She could hear some of the smaller things—beads perhaps, or marbles—falling down through the walls of the house. The house must be stuffed with all sorts of things, she thought.

"Oh, Shadow," she sighed, "what's the use?" She opened her eyes and looked into the mirror in front of her. There was still a clear space on its dusty surface where she had rubbed at it the day before.

"Hello," she said to her reflection.

The lips of the girl in the mirror moved.

Sally smoothed her skirt.

The girl in the mirror smoothed hers.

"But I'm not wearing the blue dress!" Sally said. For the girl in the mirror was. She was wearing the blue ruffled dress and the yellow bonnet, and as Sally watched, she reached down, picked up a pink parasol which lay beside her in the grass, opened it, and lifted it over her head. As she did so, Sally felt the shadow cast by the parasol spread over herself. She felt the cool slender handle in her fingers. She reached out and touched the soft grass.

The magic is happening again! she thought.

"You can sit here under the parasol with me, if you like, Patience," she said, and a very little girl in a pink pinafore, who looked a little like Emily—except that she wore long corkscrew curls rather than braids—moved over and sat next to her. She clasped her hands demurely together and looked straight ahead.

The air over the garden was perfectly still. The bright flowers stood as motionless as the seashells that lined the graveled paths winding about the garden. From time to time, an apple tree sang with the voices of the birds hidden among its leaves.

On a blanket near the two girls, in the shade of an apple tree, Bub lay sleeping on his side, one fist held tight against a closed eye. Soft bubbling sounds were rising from his mouth.

Mrs. Niminy Piminy's children, so much bigger now that they could not really be called kittens, were sleeping too, heads tucked into their curled paws. The gray one and the orange one were not far from Mrs. Niminy Piminy herself, who snoozed sedately beneath a gooseberry bush. But Tom was sleeping with his head and front paws in Elizabeth's lap, where she sat propped up against the trunk of an apple tree. For of course, he was her cat, and even slept curled up on her feet at night in the little canopied doll bed next to the fireplace in Sally's room.

Sally sighed and blew at a strand of hair that had plastered itself over her eyes. She was wearing a number of starched and scratchy petticoats, and she wished that she didn't have to entertain this shy little girl and take care of Bub besides. But her mother had asked her please to do it, so here she was, sitting in the garden, feeling hot and uncomfortable and wondering what they could do.

It seemed to Sally that all the coolness left in the world must be contained in the forest at the end of the garden. How she longed to be sitting in there on the mossy ground, with Elizabeth beside her. She would sit there and do nothing but scoop up pine needles, let them run like rain through her fingers, and listen to the ticking of the forest. She wished that at least a little of the piney coolness would blow out of the forest into the garden.

She looked at Elizabeth sitting beneath the tree, cool and unruffled while Tom purred in her lap. Elizabeth smiled serenely back at her, as if she understood everything in the world.

"Then make a breeze come, please, Elizabeth," she said aloud.

Patience looked sideways at her, without moving.

A small yellow butterfly seemed to spring from Elizabeth's bonnet, though Sally knew that it must have arrived so swiftly that she had not seen it come. It sat on the brim of the bonnet, its tissue-paper wings throbbing as if a breeze moved them. A fluttering bouquet of blue and yellow butterflies settled on a seashell near Elizabeth's feet.

Now, as if the arrival of the butterflies had been a signal, a pink flower dipped its head. A ripple ran over a bed of nasturtiums. A delphinium swayed. The whole garden woke up. Apple trees shook birds from their branches. Wind whispered in the empty seashells. Sally felt the coolness of the breeze on her hand and then on her cheek, and she sighed with pleasure. Patience, who sat with her legs straight out in front of her, wiggled her toes, as if she liked it too. Now the lilac bushes enclosing the garden stirred, and beyond them, ripple after ripple ran over the surrounding fields. The blowing foxtails and grass seemed to be hurrying toward the distant hills.

The heads of the cats lifted from their paws. Their eyes blinked. Their ears perked up. They all—except for Mrs. Niminy Piminy, who watched them through slitted eyes—leaped up and began to chase butterflies. Tom watched as the last butterfly lifted away to the sky, his tail twitching in the grass. The wind was dying down now.

Sally bobbed her head at Elizabeth. "Thank you, Elizabeth," she said.

The little doll smiled serenely back at her.

Patience spoke for the first time. "Is she magic?" she asked. Her eyes were very round.

"I don't know," said Sally, which was true.

She lowered her parasol and smiled at Patience. "Would you like to play tea party?" she asked. Patience nodded her head once. She was staring at Elizabeth.

Sally picked up the little white china teapot from the grass in front of her, and poured sugar water into one of the tiny white cups.

"Thank you," Patience whispered in a teeny-weeny voice as Sally handed the cup to her.

The cup clinked against its saucer, and there came an answering clink from the back porch, where the mothers of the two girls sat drinking real tea. The far-off murmur of their voices blended pleasantly with the drowsy buzzing of the garden.

"Oh, I've dropped it!" cried Patience, jumping to her feet. For she had spilled the sugar-water tea all over her pink pinafore. A stain was

slowly spreading over her skirt as she stood there looking down at it in dismay. Her eyes filled with tears. Her lips began to tremble.

Oh, dear, thought Sally, feeling very sorry for the little girl. "Don't cry," she begged.

"And I've broken the handle off the cup," the girl sobbed, while tears slipped out around the edges of her eyes. She pointed to where the cup lay upon its side next to a large seashell, its handle quite shattered. A blue butterfly returned for a moment to settle on the cup. Its fluttering wings cast a blue light on the thin china. The blue stain spread like a teardrop.

"Oh, that's all right," said Sally with an effort, for she dearly loved the little set and her heart felt quite as shattered as the handle. "There are lots more, and my papa can surely fix it."

Just then, Elizabeth fell over with a soft plop. Sally looked up. One of the doll's cotton hands, as she lay there, seemed to be pointing toward Tom, who was crouched, his ears flat against his head, the tip of his tail twitching. He looked just ready to spring upon a very tiny toad sitting beside the apple tree. It was hard to see the toad, because its skin so perfectly blended with the crinkly bark of the tree. It was blinking rapidly, and its throat was bulging in and out and out and in.

"Scat, Tom!" cried Sally, clapping her hands sharply. The cat jumped, gave her a baleful look, and slunk away into the gooseberry bushes.

But the toad still sat there, looking quite frozen with fear.

"Look," Sally whispered, reaching up and taking Patience's freckled hand in her own, and drawing her down next to her. "Look at the toad. I think it's just going to hop!"

The toad, with one last convulsive movement of its throat, jumped. Up, up, it went, and down—right into Sally's cup of tea.

Sally and Patience hugged each other, rocking with laughter. Bub woke up, blinked his eyes, and began to laugh too—"Salwy funny!" he crowed, pointing a fat pink finger. "Funny, funny Salwy!"

And that made them laugh even harder.

"What's happening out there?" called Sally's mother from the porch. They could see her face peering anxiously through the vines that grew up over the roof of the porch, forming a green curtain as they went.

"'S all right," gasped Sally. When she and Patience wiped their eyes and sat up at last, still weakly laughing, they saw that the toad had disappeared. All trace of the spilled sugar water had been absorbed by the thirsty dry ground. Bub was sucking his thumb and looking inquiringly at them with his clear round eyes, and Mrs. Niminy Piminy was composedly blinking her green eyes at them. Her children, except for Tom, who watched from the gooseberry bush, had all gone back to sleep.

"Please have some pumpkin pie," said Sally, offering Patience the center of a daisy upon a little china plate.

"Thank you," said Patience, and pretended to nibble at it, her eyes lowered.

Then she began to grin again. The lashes fluttered up. A last giggle shook her body. "Jumped right into the cup," she said.

"Yes," said Sally, "spilled the whole thing."

"Funny Salwy," said Bub, removing his thumb from his mouth and holding it over his head. He lay on his back, gazing up at it, as if he found his thumb most remarkable.

Sally picked Elizabeth up and straightened her bonnet. "Elizabeth saved that toad's life," she said. "Tom was just going to get it when she fell over. It looked just as if she was pointing at Tom to show me." She kissed the little doll.

"Maybe she *is* magic," breathed Patience, looking with deep respect at Elizabeth.

"Maybe," said Sally, feeling very proud of her pretty doll.

But Elizabeth just went on smiling her usual sunny smile.

Tom came padding back and warily placed his head upon Elizabeth's lap.

"Naughty Tom," Sally scolded. "But I guess you can't help it. You're just a cat. And Elizabeth seems to like you." She placed the little doll's hand on Tom's head, and Tom purred and closed his eyes.

Sally and Patience spent the rest of the afternoon quite pleasantly. Sally showed her the store of pepper boxes made from the seed containers of poppy plants that she kept in a hollow in one of the apple trees, along with some acorn cups. They sprinkled the seeds over a stew of leaves and berries they mixed together and cooked in the sun and then fed to Elizabeth. Holding Bub's hands while he toddled along between them, they pushed through a gap in the lilac bushes and sat for a time in the field, hidden from sight by the blowing foxtails. They made daisy chains while they were sitting there, from daisies they gathered by armfuls. And they made a hat for Elizabeth from a castor-bean leaf, and tied it with dandelion stems, and then they made dandelion-stem curls and hung them on their ears and tucked them beneath Elizabeth's bonnet. When Bub begged them to do so, they placed some on his ears too.

"What a pretty girl you'd be, Bub," said Sally.

"P'etty gi'l," Bub crowed.

Then, holding Bub's hands again, and leaving Elizabeth behind in the garden with the cats, they even went into the cool-smelling woods. They surprised a rabbit, who jumped across their path, scattering pine needles as it went. Its white tail flashed as it vanished into the green darkness beyond the sunny clearing in which they stood.

When Bub began to cry with tiredness, they took him back to the garden and, rather tired themselves, flopped down on the grass and made hollyhock dolls, with twigs for arms. They danced the dolls about by blowing on them, to amuse Bub.

Meantime, the shadows were growing longer, till at last they could scarcely see each other at all. The bright roses seemed to be floating on the soft darkness, the white ones shining like moons. Their sweetness spilled over into the garden. Sally yawned and stretched. Patience's eyes were drooping. Bub was crying again.

The footsteps of Sally's and Patience's mothers crunched on the graveled path. Their long skirts whispered over the grass, ballooned over the seashells, and scattered little pieces of gravel.

"Time to go home," said Patience's mother.

"Time to go in," said Sally's mother, and she picked Bub up and kissed his fat, warm neck.

"Please, may I light the gas plant first?" begged Sally.

Her mother sighed. "All right," she said, patting Bub's shoulder and then placing him on the ground once more. He gave a loud sniff and began to suck his thumb.

Her mother reached into her pocket, took out a match, and bent to strike it on a stone. She handed the little torch to Sally. Sally took it, and turned to the tall plant that grew at the edge of the path, its white flowers expectantly open, its pointed leaves upright and alert as cats' ears. All around her Sally could feel the watching eyes gleaming in the dark: Bub's, Patience's, the cats', and perhaps, from beneath a leaf somewhere, the little hoptoad's. Gently, she touched the match to each bloom. Up leaped a tiny bluish flame till the entire plant trembled with its own light.

"Oooh," came the whispers from all sides. "Oooh."

Beneath the plant, a family of ladybugs of all sizes, some so tiny that they could scarcely be seen in the wavering light, scattered in all directions.

And something else showed too.

"Tom!" cried Sally.

"Oh, for goodness' sake!" said her mother, laughing. "That cat!"

For in the glow of the gas plant, Tom's pointed face loomed from underneath a gooseberry bush. He had Elizabeth in his mouth. Her bonnet was all askew, her arms and legs were dangling, and her face, looking quite pathetically helpless, hung upside down.

"Put her down, Tom!" Sally ordered, making a threatening dart at him.

Tom flicked a cross green glance at Sally, dropped the doll, and began to nibble at his paws, by way of cleaning them.

Sally straightened Elizabeth's bonnet and adjusted her dress. "Honestly," she said. "I think he was going to hide her somewhere! I think he really believes she belongs to him! Naughty Tom!"

Tom blinked and mewed sleepily.

The flames of the gas plant flickered out.

"Time to go in."

Someone had lit the lamps inside the house, and the light streamed out through the porch vines into the garden. The white glimmer of the seashells led them along the path.

Sally, hugging Elizabeth, followed the others into the house.

Gingerbread Cookies

TO SALLY'S IMMENSE SURPRISE, Elizabeth, as she hugged her, gave a little squeal. But of course it was not Elizabeth at all, but poor Shadow, who had curled up in Sally's lap and gone to sleep, and been awakened by that fierce, if loving, hug.

"Oh, Shadow," said Sally, scratching his ear where he most loved to have it scratched. "I'm sorry. I was dreaming again. But how funny! Both my dreams have been about things that the other Sally wrote about in her diary." She looked back into the mirror, but she saw only Shadow and herself reflected there now.

"But do you know something, Shadow?" she whispered into his ear. "They don't seem exactly like dreams. It almost seems as if they're really happening. And look," she said, remembering something and reaching into her pocket, "this must be a piece of one of the shells from the garden. The shells in the cupboard used to be out there." She stared in awe at the bit of shell in her hand, feeling almost as if she had brought a bit of the past back with her.

Shadow reached up a paw and scratched his ear.

"But I still haven't found Elizabeth," she said unhappily, putting the shell back in her pocket. "I wonder if I ever will?"

As she was walking down the hall stairs, followed by Shadow, Sally noticed that the rain had stopped and that the sun had come out. Each trembling raindrop clinging to the window held a tiny curled rainbow. Their dancing reflections played over the stairs and along the stairway wall. She found that her gloomy gray mood of the morning had completely vanished along with the rain.

"Well," said her aunt when she walked into the kitchen. "Have you found Elizabeth yet?"

"Not yet," said Sally.

Her aunt brought a large earthenware bowl out of the cupboard and placed it on the counter. She was wearing a white apron over her dress.

"How would you like to ask your new friend to help us make gingerbread cookies?" asked Aunt Sarah.

"My friend—do you mean Emily?"

"The little girl who was with you in the sleigh."

"Oh," said Sally, remembering how Emily had disappeared. "I don't know if she—I mean,

140

I don't know if her mother will let her."

"There's only one way to find out," said Aunt Sarah briskly. "Ask her. That is, if you'd like her to come. You might have lunch together too, if you like."

"Oh, I *would* like it!" cried Sally. "But—"

"Run along, then, and ask her."

Sally hesitated for just a moment, and then she hurried out into the garden. She looked up at Emily's window. The shade was drawn again. Maybe they're not home, she told herself.

"Emily," she called, then louder, "Emily!"

With a brisk snap, the shade flew up and Emily's face appeared in the window. Her braids dangled over the sill as she leaned out. The corners of her mouth turned up in the curly smile Sally already knew so well. "Hi, Sally," she said.

"Hi, Emily, how are you?"

"I'm fine. I was just hoping you'd come out today."

"You were?" asked Sally. "But I thought—I mean, yesterday, you were gone when I came back."

"I had to go," said Emily. "My mother called me. We went shopping."

"Oh," breathed Sally. She smiled her happy relief up at her friend.

"Sally," asked Emily in an anxious voice, "are

you—will you be going home? Is your mother coming?"

Sally shook her head. "No," she said, "I told her I wanted to stay."

"Oh, I'm glad!" cried Emily. "I'm *so* glad!"

"I'm glad too," said Sally.

"Did you find Elizabeth yet?"

Sally shook her head. "Not yet," she said. "But Emily, my aunt Sarah told me to ask you if you could come over for lunch. We'll make gingerbread cookies too. Could you? Do you think your mother would let you?"

"I'd like to," said Emily eagerly. "I'll ask my mother. Wait just a minute."

Sally chewed on the end of a blade of grass while she waited. "Oh I hope," she whispered, "I hope she can." She crossed her fingers. Like a good omen from the past, a tiny toad hopped by, looking very much like the one in her dream, and vanished into the tall grass.

Emily's face showed again at the window with the suddenness of a puppet appearing on-stage. She was smiling. "My mother says I can come," she announced, and then the stage was empty. The curtains stirred a little.

Aunt Sarah had a little starched apron, white with borders of lace, for each of them, and they helped each other tie the sashes in back. "They

142

were mine when I was about your age," said Aunt Sarah.

When the cookies were baked, they ate them for dessert after their lunch of peanut-butter sandwiches, carrot sticks, and potato chips. They sat for this meal at the round table in the dining room. In the afternoon, Aunt Sarah left them to their own devices for the most part, but when she was with them, she did not seem frightening in the least, and Sally felt quite proud of her. She's *my* aunt Sarah, she thought, and she enjoyed showing her off a bit to Emily. Showing Emily about the house after lunch was like living again through the wonder of seeing it for the first time herself, only without the fear.

"Oh, there's the melodeon!" exclaimed Emily as they went into the parlor. "And it does play a little tune when you walk!" They amused themselves for a time by walking back and forth, just to hear it tinkle.

Of course, Emily had to look at the shells, and hear about how they had once lined the garden paths, and finger with wonder the bit of shell from Sally's pocket. Emily seemed quite enchanted with the frail little cups and saucers, and her eyes were like saucers themselves as she listened to Sally's story of how the handle on one of the cups had come to be broken.

"I wonder if it really did happen that way,"

said Emily, staring at the cup through their two reflections in the glass front of the cupboard.

"That's what it says in the diary," said Sally.

"Could I see the diary?" asked Emily.

Sally nodded and led the way through the bead curtains.

"Shadow's coming too," said Emily.

"Oh, he always follows me, don't you, Shadow?" said Sally. She felt quite as if this were her own home, and as though she had lived here all her life.

"What funny curtains," said Emily. "They tickle when you walk through them. Oh, look at Shadow! He slipped on that rug!" She laughed.

"Cats," said Sally, picking him up to comfort him, "are very dignified and don't like to be laughed at." And then she began to laugh.

"What's the matter?" asked Emily.

"Oh, nothing," Sally answered. "Just something I thought of."

"What a nice angel," said Emily, stopping to admire her. She touched the angel's foot, and smiled up at Sally. "I like this house," she said. "And what a long stairway. It goes on and on!"

In the upstairs hall she stared in awe at the grandfather clock, and admired the flowers on the rug. "It looks like a garden up here," she said.

Sally took her proudly into her bedroom.

"What a pretty room!" cried Emily, her eyes shining. "It's the prettiest room I ever saw! Oh, Sally, you're so lucky!"

Maybe I am, thought Sally, remembering how she had felt when she had first come here. And now—why, now she was having the best adventure of her life! How funny, she thought. If I hadn't come here, I wouldn't have known Emily, and I wouldn't know about the other Sally, and Elizabeth!

"Is that the other Sally and Elizabeth?" Emily was pointing to the picture over the fireplace.

Sally nodded.

"She *does* look just like you! And Elizabeth is—she's wonderful! Oh, Sally, you just have to find her! Wouldn't it be fun to play with her?"

Sally took Emily up to the attic and showed her the other Sally's trunk and all the things inside. She let her read the diary, and she put on the other Sally's clothes for her. She told Emily all about her dreams, and how it had seemed that she could see the other Sally in the mirror. The two of them stood side by side looking into the mirror. "Yes," said Emily, "that does look just like the other Sally in there." She took a bite from the gingerbread cookie she had brought to the attic with her. "I wish I could have a dream like that," she said wistfully.

But this time, nothing happened.

And they looked and looked for some clue to Elizabeth's whereabouts. But for a very long time they found nothing at all.

"What's Shadow doing?" asked Emily.

Sally looked up from the paper-lace valentine she had found in a box. "Oh, he's pushing something into that space between the wall and the roof. See where it comes down there? He's always doing that."

"Cats are funny," said Emily. "Is it true that they don't like to be laughed at?"

"That's what my aunt Sarah says," Sally answered, smoothing the lace of the valentine and placing it back in the box. "She's very old and she probably knows a lot."

Emily had disappeared behind a chest of drawers.

Sally looked up when she heard a gasp of surprise, which seemed, since she could not see Emily, to come from the chest itself.

"Sally!" cried Emily's excited voice. "Come here!" Her face, which to Sally's surprise had turned a glowing pink since she had last seen it, appeared briefly from behind the chest and then vanished again.

Sally was on her feet immediately, hurrying over to Emily, hardly daring to hope, scarcely able to breathe. "Is it—Elizabeth?" she whispered.

"No," said Emily, looking up at her from where she was kneeling on the floor behind the chest. "It's this!" And with a triumphant flourish she held something up in one hand.

It was Sally's turn to gasp. "Emily," she whispered. "It's Elizabeth's bonnet!"

Emily nodded her head up and down several times in rapid succession, her grin widening all the while, till it stretched almost to her ears.

Sally's trembling fingers reached out to take the little yellow bonnet. "It really is!" she cried, looking down at Emily, whose head was still bobbing excitedly up and down. "Where did you find it?"

Emily's head was slowing down, though the grin remained. "Right here," she said proudly, pointing to a spot on the dusty floor near her knees.

Sally stared at the spot as if she expected it to tell her something. There was a pounding in her ears which would have made it impossible to hear anything however, particularly the faint voice of a dust-laden floor.

She looked up at Emily. "I looked back here yesterday," she said, "and I'm sure it wasn't here then."

Emily was not smiling now. Her eyes were very dark and round with astonishment. The two girls stared at each other. They could hear

the steady ticking of the grandfather clock, like the beating of the heart of the old house. And indeed, at that moment, the house did seem to Sally to be alive, and more than that, to *know* something, about Elizabeth and the other Sally, about herself and Aunt Sarah. Houses must get to know something, she thought, with all the things that happen in them. Was it trying to tell her something?

"But how did it get here, then?" Emily was asking.

Sally shook her head. How *had* the bonnet gotten here, where it had certainly not been yesterday? She looked up at the dusty rafters overhead, not so far overhead at this point, for they were sitting only a little distance from the part of the wall where the roof sloped steeply down. By standing on tiptoe, she was able to touch the roof. She ran her fingers along the top of the rafter. The thick coating of dust that she found there had certainly not been disturbed in many years. There was nothing up there but dust. The bonnet could not have fallen down from there.

She sat down again. "Emily," she said, "do you realize what this means? It means that Elizabeth *is* here somewhere. I was right!"

Emily nodded. Her eyes were very shiny.

Sally got down on her hands and knees and

peered beneath the chest of drawers. She sat up. "She's not there," she said. She looked down at the faded little bonnet in the palm of her hand. It looked in that unsteady hand as if it were trembling with a life of its own.

As she gazed at it, her longing to find Elizabeth, to hold her in her arms, grew, until it filled her entire body and spilled over into the attic. It seemed to her that the very cobwebs shuddered in sympathy. The trunks looked as if they were about to fling open their tops in excitement.

"Emily," she said, looking up at her friend, "it almost seems as if Elizabeth is leaving clues for us, doesn't it?"

Emily touched her tongue to her upper lip and nodded. "Maybe she really is magic," she said.

"Maybe she wants us to find her," said Sally. "Maybe she's lonely."

"Yes," agreed Emily, clasping her hands tightly together and shivering with delight. "Do you think she's playing a game with us?"

Sally thought for a moment. "No," she said at last, "I don't think so. I think it's just that she can't do everything for us. We have to do something to find her." It seemed to her as she spoke that she knew Elizabeth very well, knew that she would not play such a game with them, would never tease them. Or was it the other

Sally she knew so well? After all, it was the other Sally who had first imagined things with Elizabeth, just as Sally herself was doing.

"But what can we do?" asked Emily.

"We can start looking all over again," said Sally. Determination strengthened her voice. She stood up and slipped the little hat carefully into her pocket.

Once more they made a careful search of the attic.

"She isn't here anywhere," wailed Emily at last, turning her dust-streaked face to Sally. Cobwebs were clinging to her long braids, and there was a black smudge on her nose. "Your face is all dirty, Sally," she said.

Sally nodded wearily. "There's nowhere else to look," she agreed and brushed at her cheek. But Elizabeth had to be somewhere, she reminded herself, touching the little bonnet in her pocket. Yes, she had to be.

They went downstairs to show their find to Aunt Sarah, who could not seem to believe that she held the little bonnet in her trembling fingers. She was looking at it as if it were a small ghost.

"Elizabeth *was* wearing the bonnet when she was lost, wasn't she?" asked Sally anxiously, for she had just realized that maybe the bonnet had never been lost at all. And that would mean—

that would mean that Elizabeth was as far away as ever!

But Aunt Sarah nodded. "I'm certain that she was," she answered firmly, and Sally believed her. "You say the bonnet wasn't there yesterday?" she asked.

Sally shook her head. "I know it wasn't there. I looked. I remember looking in that very place."

"It's very strange," said Aunt Sarah, "very strange indeed." And she gave the bonnet back to Sally, handling it very gently as she did so. "Wouldn't it be funny," she said, as if she were talking to herself, "if you *did* find Elizabeth after all these years?" She smiled, though it looked to Sally—she thought that she must be mistaken—as if there were *tears* in Aunt Sarah's eyes!

It was hard to say good-bye to Emily that day, for both of them were so excited that they wanted to go on and on talking about the bonnet, and how it could have come to be there on the floor of the attic, and where else they could look for Elizabeth. Even Aunt Sarah was caught up in their enthusiasm, and seemed reluctant to have it end.

"You're very sure," she said, "that you looked everywhere?" They nodded.

"Well," said Aunt Sarah at last, "maybe after dinner and a good night's sleep, you'll think of something."

"May we look again tomorrow?" Sally asked her aunt as Emily was leaving.

"Of course," said Aunt Sarah. "And Emily's invited to come again and stay for lunch."

Emily uttered a little crow of delight and leaped from the top porch step to the path, her braids flying. This reminded Sally of the famous leap of the hoptoad into the teacup, and made her laugh. She and Aunt Sarah stood companionably watching Emily skip down the path to the gate.

"Thank you, Aunt Sarah," said Sally when the gate had closed behind Emily.

"You're very welcome, Sally. Look, doesn't Shadow look happy?" said her aunt, pointing to where he was sitting on the hall rug. "I think he likes having children in the house. It livens it up. Yes, it does seem as if this old house is coming alive again."

Sally remembered how she had felt in the attic, as if the house were alive. "Do you really think houses can come alive?" she asked.

"I do," said Aunt Sarah, "when there are people in them who care for one another." And to Sally's immense surprise, Aunt Sarah bent down and kissed her on the cheek! Sally was too dumbfounded to do anything but stand there, fingering the little bonnet in her pocket and feeling, for some reason, completely happy.

She went to sleep that night, the bonnet on the night table next to her bed, feeling sure somehow that the next day she and Emily would find Elizabeth at last.

But it was not to be.

Christmas Eve

NEXT MORNING, SALLY WOKE feeling extremely strange. Her throat was now very sore, and she felt hot and cold by turns and quite horribly weak besides. When her aunt came in to say good morning, Sally found to her surprise that her own voice came out as a hoarse croak.

"My goodness," said Aunt Sarah, peering down at her. "You look terrible, Sally—all flushed and odd." She placed a gentle hand on Sally's forehead. "Why, you're simply burning up. You stay right here in bed. I'll call the doctor right away, and then I'll bring your breakfast up to you."

Sally felt as if she could not possibly do anything but stay there in bed. It was an effort even to move a finger, which she tried to do by way of greeting Shadow, who stood up, when Aunt Sarah had bustled out, from where he had been curled at her feet. He came and sat on her pillow, and licked her hot cheek with his rough tongue.

"Hi, Shadow," she croaked. "That feels good."

Sally ate scarcely any breakfast at all, and her

aunt looked worried as she carried the tray away.

Sally looked sleepily and fondly at Shadow, who was now sitting on her stomach, cleaning industriously between the toes of his paw.

"Shadow!" she cried, and she would have raised her head if it had not made her dizzy even to think of it.

Was she dreaming? For it looked to her as if Shadow had a tiny golden thread caught between the curving ivory claws of his paw—a golden thread that looked as if it must be, as if it could only be, a strand of Elizabeth's own hair! Her eyes flicked over to the bonnet on the night table, but she was sure that it had not been disturbed. The frayed ribbons still lay in the patterns she remembered from the night before.

"Shadow, let me see!" she begged, reaching a hand toward him. But Shadow stood up, stretched, and flowed smoothly as a spill of water to the floor and disappeared beneath the bed.

When Sally tried to sit up, she found that she was indeed too dizzy and exhausted to do anything but call, in a plaintive trembling whisper, "Here, Shadow, here, kitty, kitty, nice Shadow—"

She could hear him busily licking himself beneath the bed.

When Aunt Sarah returned to say that the doctor would be coming soon, Sally told her in a weak voice, which shook with excitement, about her discovery.

Aunt Sarah, listening, touched her forehead. "You're very hot," she said. "Are you sure you weren't dreaming?"

Sally tiredly shook her head from side to side. "Please, Aunt Sarah, look at Shadow's paw. He's under the bed. He *knows* where Elizabeth is!"

Aunt Sarah sighed and shook her head. She looked very worried and did not seem to be taking Sally's story seriously at all.

"Please," begged Sally.

"All right, Sal," she said, "if it'll make you feel better. Shadow!" she ordered sharply. "Come here!"

Shadow appeared, blinking, from beneath the bed. Aunt Sarah, with some difficulty, stooped to pick him up. She placed him on the bed.

"There," she said. "Where is this thread now?" Breathing hard from her exertions, she sat down on the bed next to Sally.

"On that paw," said Sally, weakly pointing.

Aunt Sarah gently lifted Shadow's right paw and peered at it. "I can't see anything," she said.

Sally stared at the paw, at the black velvety pads, at the tips of the ivory claws just showing.

"Neither can I," she said. "Maybe—maybe it was the other paw."

But, as Sally had feared, there was nothing on the other paw either.

"Now, Sal," said Aunt Sarah, after a long silence during which they did not look at each other. "I want you to rest. Forget about Elizabeth and just concentrate on getting better. You're sick, and all this excitement about the doll—I blame myself. I ought never to have let you start it—"

"But I know it was there," Sally said. "I wasn't

dreaming. He could have pulled it off when he was cleaning his paw—" Her voice trailed off into a tired mumble. Her eyes closed with weariness, and she felt a tear slip from beneath the lid of one of them and slide down her cheek.

"Sal, Sal," whispered her aunt, stroking her forehead. "Go to sleep, dear. Rest."

Aunt Sarah's cool hand felt good on her forehead, and Sally could feel herself drifting into sleep . . . slowly, slowly . . . she seemed to be sinking deeper and deeper into the soft bed. From somewhere far away, the grandfather clock whispered. Tick . . . a long pause . . . tock. Tick. . . tock.

Aunt Sarah was tiptoeing away from her bed.

But Sally was not quite asleep. She doesn't believe me, she thought.

"Does . . . n't," echoed the clock.

Her thoughts followed Aunt Sarah's footsteps along the hall.

She thinks . . . I . . . dreaming . . . Tick . . . tock. But I wasn't.

Was . . . n't.

Saw . . . thread.

Saw . . .

But Sally was asleep and did not hear the clock whisper "thread" to the empty hall.

She woke to see what at first looked like a faraway round moon hovering over her bed.

But it was, after all, Dr. Green, who turned out to be a pleasant red-faced man. He sat on her bed and petted Shadow while Sally held the thermometer in her mouth.

"Now, young lady," he said, winking at her. "You're going to be right here in bed for a few days, it seems. You have a touch of the flu that's going around, and you're not going to feel like doing much else."

A few days! What about Elizabeth? she wondered in anguish. Would she have time to find her? What about the last entry in the diary? A few days could mean a week, and then she'd probably be going home, and Aunt Sarah would sell the house, and she'd never find Elizabeth!

The doctor took the thermometer from her mouth and looked at it. He nodded. "Feverish all right," he said. "But there's no need for your aunt to get in touch with your parents. No need at all to worry them. You'll get along just fine. Just a few days in bed, and take your medicine regularly, and you'll be up and hopping around again." He stood up. "And you've done your aunt a world of good being here. She's a new person," he said.

"I feel like a new person," said Aunt Sarah. "I feel quite young again."

"Well, to make sure we keep you that way,"

said Dr. Green, "I'll send over a woman my wife knows to do a little of the heavy work while this girl's in bed."

And he and Aunt Sarah left the room.

Sally, for a day or so, slept a good deal of the time. Aunt Sarah brought medicine to her and notes from Emily, who had come to look for Elizabeth and been told that Sally was sick.

Emily's notes were truly bright spots in Sally's days. They were decorated with crayon pictures of Elizabeth, and of Sally herself holding Elizabeth and showing her to Emily, who had braids that reached to her toes, upraised hands, and a round "O" for a mouth. There was also a large one of Shadow. Aunt Sarah thought it looked just like him. She pinned all the pictures up on the wall where Sally could look at them.

Dr. Green kept his promise to send someone to help Aunt Sarah. Mrs. Binneky was a brisk, happy little person who called Sally "Love" and sang as she dusted her bedroom. One day she brought her a pink cupcake with a sugar bird on top in a crinkled green paper cup.

When Sally grew a little stronger and was able to sit up, Aunt Sarah brought her books to read and paper dolls to cut out. Sometimes they just talked together, mostly about California, which Sally had never seen. Aunt Sarah told her about the palm trees that grew along the street where she lived. "Sometimes," she said, "when you're walking along, a date will fall right on your head." And she could pick oranges and bananas from trees in her back yard. "I just reach out the window in the morning," said Aunt Sarah.

"You must like California a lot," said Sally rather wistfully.

"It's a very interesting place to live," agreed Aunt Sarah.

"I suppose you want to go back as soon as you can," said Sally.

"Well, I only came here to sell the house."

"I wonder," said Sally, "if another girl will live here."

"Oh, I don't think so," said Aunt Sarah. "It's the apartment owners who are interested in buying the house, for expansion."

"Expansion?" asked Sally. The word felt strange to her tongue. She didn't like the way it felt at all. "What do you mean?"

"Well, they want to make the apartment buildings larger, you see."

"You mean," cried Sally, "they'd tear the house down?"

"I'm afraid so," said Aunt Sarah.

Sally's lips began to tremble. Her eyes filled with tears.

"Why, Sally," said her aunt, taking her hand. "Do you like this old house so much?"

Sally gulped and nodded.

"I wish you didn't have to sell it," she whispered.

But her aunt only patted her hand and said nothing.

Then one day Emily was allowed to come in and sit by her bed in the little blue chair, and they talked about everything, about Elizabeth, and Emily's little brother, Richard, who was only a baby. "I take care of him," said Emily proudly, and Sally told her about Bub and how funny he was. Aunt Sarah, to their delight, brought up the little tea set, including the broken-handled cup, and they had a tea party like the one in the long-ago garden, with sugar water for tea.

Emily said that when Sally was better her mother wanted her to come over to her house and play, and then she could see Richard, and they made plans to visit each other after Sally had gone home.

"But I won't be staying here," said Sally unhappily, looking around the pretty room and thinking how much she had grown to love it. She told Emily about how the house would be torn down.

"They *can't* do that!" gasped Emily, and her eyes filled with tears just as Sally's had.

"But don't worry," Emily said kindly at last,

wiping her eyes. "We'll play at my house. We'll play with Elizabeth."

But Sally shook her head sadly. "I don't think I'm going to find her," she said. "I'm not going to have time. I'll be going back to school, and Aunt Sarah will go back to California, and the house will be—gone."

"Oh, but you will find her!" cried Emily, looking up at the picture. "I just know you will. I'd feel awful if you didn't."

"So would I," Sally agreed.

But at last the day came when she was well enough to get out of bed and go downstairs for breakfast.

"It's so good to have you up and about," said her aunt, smiling at her.

"It's good to be up," said Sally. Then, "Aunt Sarah," she said, "do you think I could go up to the attic today?"

Her aunt said nothing for a time. She seemed to be thinking. She looked closely at Sally. "I don't know," she said at last. "I thought perhaps you ought to play outside—but it is a little chilly. Oh, I suppose if you're sure you feel all right, it won't hurt you. Go ahead."

"Oh, thank you!" And off Sally went once more to the attic, followed by her faithful Shadow.

How wonderful the attic looked to her after her long absence! It seemed indeed to welcome

165

her. The little brass label on the other Sally's trunk winked a greeting at her. It seemed to be speaking right to her, just as it had on the first day she had seen it. But she passed by the trunk and went straight to the mirror.

She sat down in front of the mirror, feeling suddenly quite out of breath, and she remembered that she had just gotten over being sick. "There's a sort of ringing in my ears," she told herself, closing her eyes. For there was a faint jingling sound, rather like the sound of far-off sleigh bells. "Jingle bells, jingle bells," she whispered. No, it seemed as if someone were singing—no, whistling—somewhere, someone was whistling "Jingle Bells," and there *were* bells ringing!

Oh, my, she thought, I must still be sick. Her head was spinning. She felt quite dizzy.

And then she opened her eyes and saw the other Sally in the mirror. There was no mistaking her this time.

She was wearing a little red velvet cape with a pointed hood that covered her hair entirely. Her hands were tucked into a white fur muff just like the one Elizabeth carried in the picture. The little doll was seated upon her lap, and she too was wearing a tiny red-hooded cape. Snow was swirling about them, and there were snowflakes on their hoods and even clinging to the other Sally's eyelashes. And how dark it was; the stars looked as if they were falling too, all mixed up with the twirling of the snowflakes.

How cozy it feels, thought Sally, snuggling down into the fur rug which covered her knees and the knees of her mother, who sat beside her. Sally stuck out her tongue and caught a cold snowflake on its tip.

They were riding in the red sleigh, the sleigh bells ringing as they glided over the glittering snow. Her father was seated on the driver's seat high above them, whistling "Jingle Bells" and gently slapping the reins in his hands on the rising and falling back of the horse, which whinnied and raised its nose to the falling snow. When the horse turned its head, Sally could see its great eye flashing in the light of the lanterns that hung on either side of the sleigh. The cloud of its frosty breath hovered in the crystal air. Up a hill they went, seeming to be flying straight toward the round moon. Sally could hear the sound of the horse's hoofs breaking through the crusty snow. Up and over the snowdrifts they flew, wind whistling past their ears. It nipped at Sally's nose and she drew her head further into the hood of her cape. Snow blew into her eyes and stiffened her lashes with cold. Snowflakes circled like moths around the lanterns, which swayed and bumped against the sides of the sleigh and cast leaping patterns of light on the banks of snow and the glittering ice-covered branches of the trees.

The branches struck a frosty music from the air above them, and Sally reached up and broke a twig from a low-hanging branch as they sped along past the lighted windows of farmhouses, past the schoolhouse and the reaching spire of the church, with the silver moon caught on its tip. The moon looks like a crystal ball tonight, thought Sally. She looked down at the icy twig she held in her mittened hand. It looked silvery, a twig from a silver tree in a fairy tale. She waved it at the wonderful moon and then let it fall from the sleigh into the snow. It seemed a night when anything could happen.

"Jingle bells, jingle bells," sang her father's deep voice, and he shook the reins and grinned around at her as the bells on the reins jingled a lively accompaniment.

"Careful, John," cried her mother in a worried voice. "We're going very fast."

"Whoa," said her father at last, standing up, the rug which covered his knees slipping over the edge of the seat as he did so. Sally reached up and caught the edge of the rug and looked up at him. "Here?" she asked.

"Right about here, I reckon," said her father, peering about. Sally could see that they had stopped at the edge of a forest. Her father threw the reins over the seat and jumped out into the snow.

"Ah, there she is," he said, lifting one of the lanterns from the sleigh and holding it so that Sally and her mother could see the fir tree, which lay on its side almost buried in the snow. "Perkins and I cut it this afternoon," he said proudly. "Couldn't bring it back then with all the wood we were carrying. But there it is—the biggest Christmas tree in the whole forest!"

"Oh it is!" breathed Sally. As she moved to look down at it, her hood fell back from her hair. She didn't notice it until her mother reached over and pulled it up. "It must be the biggest tree in the world!"

"Will it fit into the parlor?" asked her mother.

"Have to make the parlor bigger if it doesn't," said Sally's father, and accompanied by some good-natured grunting and groaning and a few more bars of "Jingle Bells," he stood the tree up, shook some of the snow from its branches, and hoisted it up onto the back of the sleigh. With some help from Sally and her mother, he secured it there with ropes.

And back they drove through the frosted air, over the moon-sparkled drifts, the lovely piney smell accompanying them all the way and reminding them, though they hardly needed a reminder, that this was indeed Christmas Eve. The church bells were chiming as they passed the little white church once more. Light streamed out onto the snow from its doorway.

Other sleighs passed them. "Merry Christmas," called the people. The fluttering ends of the shawls and scarves in which they were wrapped waved gaily as they drove by.

"Merry Christmas," they shouted in return. Patience went by with her family in their sleigh, muffled to her ears in a yellow shawl that glinted in the moonlight. "Merry Christmas, Elizabeth!" she called, and Sally held Elizabeth up and made her wave a cotton hand at her.

The tree was dragged into the house at last, along with a good deal of snow, which Sally's mother did her very best to seem stern about, rather unsuccessfully, for she was as excited as any of them.

They stood the tree up in a corner of the parlor next to the melodeon, which made a continuous tinkling comment upon the proceedings as they worked. The tree fit exactly, its tip just brushing the ceiling of the room.

"It's beautiful!" said Sally.

"Twee!" cried little Bub, and they had to hold him back, for he rushed at it on his chubby legs as if he meant to push it over, if possible, just for the fun of seeing it raised again to the ceiling. Mrs. Perkins caught him just in time. "Little dear," she cried, kissing him. "The little, little dear."

Aunt Tryphone vowed she had never seen such a tree in all her ninety-five years. "And I even doubt," she said, "that my dear papa who once spoke to Mr. Washington saw such a tree. Mr. Washington himself may not even have been so fortunate."

"Put your apron on, Sally," said her mother, "to keep your dress clean." And Sally ran to the kitchen to get her white apron with the borders of lace.

Mrs. Niminy Piminy, to everyone's surprise, for they would have believed her too dignified for such behavior, tried to climb up the tree, and like Bub, had to be restrained. Her grown-up kittens behaved much better, sitting in a line and blinking in astonishment as the tree was decorated with strings of popcorn and cranberries Sally had made with Bub's "help" during many evenings at the kitchen table, cotton-whiskered Santas, and beautiful shining balls of red and gold and green glass. There were swans and birds with feathered tails, and angel hair and tinsel and tiny red candles in silver holders. When it was all done at last, they stood back to admire it.

Sally, holding Elizabeth in her arms, was

looking especially hard at the top of the tree. Then she looked down at Elizabeth, smiled, and hugged her. "We need a Christmas angel!" she said, pointing, "at the top of the tree. Elizabeth could be our angel." And indeed, Elizabeth, her feet flying as Sally lifted her, looked as if she were already winging her way to the topmost branch of the tree.

"Ango," cried Bub, clapping his chubby hands.

They all looked fondly at Elizabeth and nodded.

"She'll make a dear little angel," agreed Mrs. Perkins.

Aunt Tryphone could be heard to murmur something about Mr. Washington and Christmas angels.

"I'll bring the ladder back," said Father.

And he did. He helped Sally climb almost to the very top of the ladder, and then he handed Elizabeth up to her.

Up there, Sally could smell the piney smell of Christmas, which is like nothing else in the world. She felt quite delightfully faint with it.

"Steady there," warned her father as she swayed, and Sally lifted Elizabeth high into the air. "Here's some string," said her father. "Can you tie her to the peak?"

Sally took the string and gently tied Elizabeth to the top of the glittering tree, and blew a kiss to her.

Sally came down again and they all stood looking up at Elizabeth.

"She's the most beautiful angel in the world," said Sally.

"Indeed she is."

"Dear little thing."

"Fing, fing."

Tom sat looking up longingly at his friend. "He wants to be up there with her," said Sally.

Her mother said, "He'd better not try to get there!"

Then, with Sally's mother playing the melodeon, they all sang Christmas carols: "Jingle Bells" and "Hark the Herald Angels Sing," and last of all, "Silent Night." And while they sang, snow fell upon the house and upon the hills and upon all the sleeping fields.

It was Sally who first saw that Elizabeth was gone.

They had stopped singing at last, too tired to go on, and they had all turned to admire the tree once more.

Sally, of course, looked for Elizabeth first of all.

"Mama!" she cried. "Elizabeth! She's gone!"

"Goodness!" cried her mother. "So she is."

"Dear little thing," said Mrs. Perkins. "No doubt she's fallen."

"But then where is she?" cried Sally, for she was looking all around the bottom of the tree and could not find her.

"In among the branches probably," said her father, bringing the ladder back once more. They searched and searched among the branches, but Elizabeth was nowhere to be found. They looked and looked, till they all knew that there was no point in looking any more.

"But where could she go?" Sally was sobbing. "She couldn't just vanish!"

They all stood looking unhappily down at Sally, not knowing what to do. Then her mother knelt beside her and took her in her arms and kissed her. "Sal," she said, "you mustn't. Elizabeth wouldn't want to spoil your Christmas, darling, you know she wouldn't."

"I know," sobbed Sally into her mother's comforting shoulder. "I know but I can't help it. I miss her so." She sniffed and looked up at her mother. "Oh, Mama," she said, "I had such good times with her."

"There, dear," comforted her mother. "Don't cry, don't cry."

Elizabeth

"DON'T CRY, SAL. DON'T CRY, there, dear."

Sally looked up to find Aunt Sarah seated on the attic floor, holding her in her arms. "Sal, Sal, what's the matter, dear?" she was saying. "You've overtired yourself. I shouldn't have let you come up here."

Sally rubbed at her eyes. "No," she said, "it's all right. I was crying about Elizabeth, when the other Sally lost her."

"There, dear, you were dreaming again," said Aunt Sarah, gently smoothing her hair back from her forehead.

"No," said Sally, shaking her head, "no, it wasn't like a dream. It was just as if it was happening. And the other Sally had an apron like yours, like the ones you had when you were a little girl."

"Did she?" murmured Aunt Sarah. She was looking off somewhere over Sally's head, as if she too could see into the past.

Sally gulped and nodded. She sat up slowly.

"Where's Shadow?" she asked.

"Up to his usual tricks," said Aunt Sarah, pointing at him. He was poking at something between the roof and the floor, poking and poking. "Aren't cats funny?"

"But they don't like to be laughed at," said Sally.

"Well," said Aunt Sarah, "perhaps they don't mind so awfully much."

"Shadow looks like Mrs. Niminy Piminy, but he looks even more like Tom."

"Old Tom," sighed Aunt Sarah.

But Sally didn't hear her. She was remembering something—the bonnet found by Emily, the golden thread in Shadow's paw and Tom, sitting under the Christmas tree, gazing up at his friend Elizabeth. Tom, who had carried Elizabeth in his mouth in the garden. What if, while they were singing, Elizabeth had fallen off the tree? What if Tom had still been sitting there, watching her? What would he have done if she had fallen to the floor? Her eyes flicked to Shadow, poking his paw into the space under the roof. What if Tom had taken Elizabeth in his mouth? What if, while they were singing, he had walked silently past them, up the stairs, and up more stairs, and what if the attic door had been open? Yes, what if Tom was like Shadow? They were both cats, weren't they?

Sally sat up very straight. Her heart was pounding as she stared at Shadow.

"What is it, Sally?" asked Aunt Sarah.

But Sally didn't answer. She jumped to her feet and ran over to Shadow. "Shadow!" she cried. "What are you doing?" Shadow looked up at her, then went on poking with his paw. She could hear him growling low in his throat. "He's trying to get something out of there," she said. She knelt beside him, pushed him gently aside, and reached into the dark space.

Her hands closed over something soft, something that made her fingertips tingle. She drew it out and held it up.

"Elizabeth!" she cried.

For it was indeed the little doll herself, muff, ruffled dress and all, dusty, rumpled, and rather dirty; but without any doubt whatsoever, dear, dear old golden-haired, sweet-smiling Elizabeth! Tears were running down Sally's cheeks onto Elizabeth's head as she hugged her and then hugged her again.

"What is it, Sally? What's wrong?" cried her aunt. And she moved so suddenly that she knocked against the mirror in passing, and it fell and broke with a crash that reverberated through the attic.

But her aunt ignored the mirror and hurried over to her. "Whatever is it, Sally?" she asked.

Sally, laughing and crying all at once, word-lessly held the doll up to her.

Aunt Sarah uttered a strange little cry of joy. She sat down on the floor. Tears ran down her wrinkled cheeks.

"It *is* Elizabeth! Sal!" she cried. "You've solved the mystery! How did you do it!"

"Shadow was trying to get her out all the time," said Sally. "He knew! He knew where Elizabeth was! He got the bonnet out, and there *was* a piece of her hair in his paw!" She stroked his fur. "Oh, Shadow, you're wonderful!"

Shadow blinked and purred his happiness, and Sally told her aunt about the dream and how she had figured out what had happened.

"Sal, this is just amazing!" said her aunt. She was holding Elizabeth out and smiling at her, just as if she knew her. "Well, old Eliza-beth," she was saying, "we'll have to wash your dress and iron it, and then we'll brush your hair, and you'll be just like your old self. And of course," she added, handing the doll back to Sally, "she's yours."

"She is?" whispered Sally, looking down in wonder at Elizabeth cradled in her arms. Elizabeth seemed to be smiling up at her. "She's mine?"

"Of course," said her aunt. "I know that the other Sally would want you to have her."

"Do you think so?" asked Sally.

"I know so."

"If only she could know," said Sally, glancing over at the broken mirror.

"I think she does," said Aunt Sarah.

"You do?"

Her aunt nodded.

Yes, thought Sally. Maybe she did. Somehow. "I think Elizabeth really is a little magic," she said.

"So do I," said her aunt. "Come, let's all go down now."

"But the mirror," said Sally.

"Never mind," said her aunt. "It doesn't matter. We'll clean it up later. We'll take care of Elizabeth first. She's been waiting a long, long time."

"The bonnet!" said Sally. She took it from her pocket and placed it on Elizabeth's head. Then they went off down the stairs together.

"May I show her to Emily?" Sally asked.

"Run along," said her aunt, smiling.

"Sally, you're better!" cried Emily, when she had come to the window in response to Sally's excited call.

Sally nodded. For a moment she could not speak.

"What are you holding behind your back, Sally?"

Sally brought the doll out and held her up.

"Elizabeth!" shrieked Emily, very nearly falling out the window. "You found her! How? Where?"

"Tom hid her in the attic," said Sally, "in the space under the roof. Shadow and I found her!"

Emily's mother, carrying little Richard in her arms, came hurrying to the window to see what was going on.

"What a lovely doll," she said, smiling down at Sally.

"Dow, Dow!" crowed Richard, waving his pink fists.

"And just think, Emily," said Sally, "you helped me to find her."

"I *did?*" gasped Emily.

"Yes, that time in the sleigh, when you said that maybe the cats knew what happened. It started me thinking. And then *you* found the bonnet!"

Emily was beaming with pride.

Of course, she came along to help wash and iron Elizabeth's clothes. When they were done, they took Elizabeth up to the bedroom and compared her with the picture. "She looks just the same."

"Maybe even better," said Emily.

"Do you think the other Sally knows?" asked Sally.

Emily looked solemnly up at the picture. "Yes," she said gravely. "Oh, Sally," she whispered, "this is the most exciting thing that ever happened to me!"

"Me too," said Sally.

That night Sally dreamed that she saw the other Sally. Sally held Elizabeth up and said, "I found her," and the other Sally smiled and waved. "I'm happy now," said the other Sally, and vanished.

Aunt Sarah

SALLY WOKE WITH ELIZABETH beside her on her pillow. "And I'm happy too," she said to the little doll. "And I really think the other Sally does know now." It seemed to her that Elizabeth was smiling just a little more than usual.

Her mother and father came to get her that day not long after breakfast. She ran down the front path to the little iron gate, Elizabeth in her arms, and threw herself into her mother's waiting arms, and then into her father's. They were all laughing and talking at once as they came up the path together. No one heard what anyone else was saying, though perhaps Sally's mother understood what had happened because Sally kept waving Elizabeth excitedly beneath her nose. At least, she understood it all later, when they had calmed down a little.

Aunt Sarah was waiting in the doorway with Shadow as they came up onto the porch. Sally's mother ran to her and kissed her.

"Aunt Sal!" she cried, hugging her. "Oh, Aunt Sal!"

Sally stopped in astonishment and stared at them. "What did you say?"

Her mother turned and smiled at her. "I said, 'Aunt Sal.' I haven't seen Aunt Sal in years and years, and I'm so glad to see her!"

"What's the matter, Sally?" asked her father.

For Sally was staring at her aunt. Aunt Sarah's eyes were twinkling, and her lips were twitching a little, as if a smile were trying to get out.

"But you're Aunt *Sarah!*" she said.

Her aunt nodded. "But my nickname was always Sal."

Sally stared some more. Then she said slowly, "You're—you're the other Sally! And Elizabeth was yours! You knew about her, and about Mrs. Niminy Piminy—"

Her aunt nodded. She was *really* smiling now.

"Oh, Aunt Sarah!" cried Sally, and she rushed into her aunt's arms, Elizabeth and all. "I love you," she said, kissing her aunt's cheek.

"And I love you, Sal," said her aunt.

"And I'd love to get inside," said her father, "if you two Sallys will let me by."

They all went into the parlor and talked and talked. The melodeon, of course, joined in from time to time.

"And so," said her father at last, "you'll be

selling the old house and going back to California, will you? It looks to me as if Sally here is going to miss you."

Aunt Sarah smiled and shook her head. "I've changed my mind."

They all looked at her.

"You see," she explained, looking down at her hands in her lap, "I really felt just terrible about selling this old place, and maybe having them tear it down, but there seemed to be no reason not to—now there are lots of them." She placed her arms on the arms of the chair and looked fondly over at Sally. "I love this old house. I'm an old lady and it's full of my memories. I'll come here every summer and go to California for the winter, if I feel like it. I'd like to have the garden fixed up, put all these shells along the paths again, and have the house painted. Yes, I'm staying. That is, if Sally and Elizabeth will come to visit me from time to time."

"Oh, Aunt Sarah," whispered Sally, and her eyes were shining with what might have been tears. "I'm so glad! I can't wait to tell Emily!"

"And will you come?" asked her aunt.

"Oh, yes!" cried Sally. "Yes, we will!"

And they did.